"What are you [...] afraid of, Lesl[...]

Oliver's eyes roved [...] turned stubbornly toward th[...]. But he gave a gentle tug and pulled her down onto the sand, into his arms. "Now," he murmured, "look at me and tell me what's on your mind."

"You!" Leslie cried. "You! You shouldn't be here, Oliver Ames. You're all wrong for me. I need...." Her voice trailed off as the damp warmth of his skin enveloped her. "I need...."

"I know what you need," Oliver whispered. "You need a man's loving." He pressed his lips to her throat as she gave a convulsive swallow, then moved his body over hers. "You need me...."

Dear Reader,

We at Harlequin are extremely proud to introduce
our new series, **HARLEQUIN TEMPTATION**.
Romance publishing today is exciting, expanding
and innovative. We have responded to the ever-
changing demands of you, the reader, by creating
this new, more sensuous series. Between the covers
of each **HARLEQUIN TEMPTATION** you will find
an irresistible story to stimulate your imagination
and warm your heart.

Styles in romance change, and these highly
sensuous stories may not be to every reader's taste.
But Harlequin continues its commitment to
satisfy all your romance-reading needs with
books of the highest quality. Our sincerest wish is
that **HARLEQUIN TEMPTATION** will bring you
many hours of pleasurable reading.

THE EDITORS

U.S.
HARLEQUIN TEMPTATION
2504 WEST SOUTHERN AVE.
TEMPE, ARIZONA
85282

CAN.
HARLEQUIN TEMPTATION
P.O. BOX 2800
POSTAL STATION "A"
WILLOWDALE, ONTARIO
M2N 5T5

A Special Something

BARBARA DELINSKY

Harlequin Books

TORONTO • NEW YORK • LONDON
AMSTERDAM • PARIS • SYDNEY • HAMBURG
STOCKHOLM • ATHENS • TOKYO • MILAN

Published March 1984

ISBN 0-373-25104-1

Printed in Canada

Hello?

How's America's answer to Michelangelo?

Feeling more like a frustrated David.

After last night?

After this morning. I was hoping to wake up with you in my arms. What time did you leave?

Just after dawn. You were sleeping so soundly I didn't have the heart to disturb you.

Some lover. Leaves me all alone to fight the Monday-morning blues wearing nothing but a bedsheet and the very last of my Homme Premier cologne.

Mmm. Sounds enticing.

That's the point. When will you be back?

Tomorrow night. What would you like from New Orleans?

Just you. Dressed in soft pink. With a silky white negligee in your bag. And . . . darling?

Yes?

Bring a bottle of Homme Premier, will you? No David should be without it.

Rogue!

Fascinated, Leslie Parish stared at the advertisement for a long time. He was magnificent, this one whose lover had deserted him at dawn. A sculptor, his tools lay scattered atop the distant workbench at the base of a half-finished piece of art. A man, his studio apartment was a blend of muted browns and charcoals and sunlit whites. A lover, his bed was large and strewn with a sensual array of sheets barely covering one leg, and that part David hadn't tried to hide. Again and again Leslie's gaze returned to the taunting strip of flesh at his hip. Sucking in a wistful breath, she let her eye creep back up, over the broad and sinewed expanse of his lightly haired chest to his face.

Dark wavy hair, mussed by sleep, fell across his brow. His jaw bore the faintest shadow of a beard. His nose was straight; his lips firm, slightly parted. But what intrigued her most was the expression that the camera's soft lens had captured as he'd stared into his dreams with the phone cradled against his ear. A moment of vulnerability, an exquisite blend of lonely and loving that reached out to every woman on earth who had ever glimpsed a masterpiece and craved to touch it. . . .

"That's a crock!" The angry voice of Anthony Parish suddenly filled the room, startling her from her reverie, bringing her head sharply up. Her brother's hand gripped the phone, and his good-looking features were harsh in contrast to those of the face beneath her fingertips. "I don't care *how* long it takes to substantiate those facts! I'm paying top dollar and I want results!" He cast a glance at Leslie, then shook his head. "No, no. Not that way. Listen, you work on it. I'll be in touch later."

Replacing the receiver, he pushed himself from his chair and rounded the desk to take the seat beside her. Despite the flecks of gray that whispered through his hair, he was tall and lean, carrying his forty years well. "Sorry about that, Les," he murmured, "but someone's got to keep on top of them."

"I thought you had assistants to handle things like that."

Steepling his fingers, he leaned forward with a sigh.

"The buck stops here. If I want this publishing house to make it in a struggling economy, it's *my* responsibility. Quality is the name of the game. At least for me it is. I want every story we print to be right." He shot a glance at the magazine that lay open on Leslie's lap. "*Man's Mode* has done well precisely because it's a notch above." He sighed again. "But that's not your worry—" he sent her a teasing smile "—unless you'd like to change your mind and join us."

Leslie held up a slender hand. "No, thanks. I rather like being the black sheep of the family. I mean, you've got the publishing end and Diane's got sporting goods and Brenda's tied up in computers, while dad sits up there as chairman of the board. No," she smiled, "I'll stick to my kids."

Teasing yielded to a moment's admiration. "You love your work, don't you?"

"Um hmm."

"I'm glad, Les. Hey!" The rotating file in Tony's mind must have given a sudden flip. "You've got a birthday coming up."

"Um hmm."

"A big one."

She'd been trying to forget. "Um hmmmmm."

"What do you want?"

She crinkled up her nose. "Nothing. Really."

"Come on. It's not every day that a woman turns thirty."

"Thank God."

"Leslie," her brother chided, "you're not feeling your age, are you? Hell, self-made woman and all, you're doing better than ever."

On the surface she was. Inside, though, there was a growing sense of restlessness. "I suppose," she said thoughtfully.

"So what's your pleasure?" He sat back in his chair

and eyed her speculatively. "A watch? Better still—" his brown eyes lit up "—how about a fur jacket? Something soft and chic?"

"Really, Tony. I don't want anything. . . ."

He arched a brow. "I won't take no for an answer. You may be a successful professional, but you're still my little sister. In my book, that gives me the right to dote. So," he breathed, as though the matter was settled, "what'll it be? For your thirtieth—a special something. . . ."

Leslie thought for a minute. Her gaze dropped to the advertisement that still lay open on her lap. Her forefinger traced the swath of skin whose lightly bronzed color ran unbroken from head to foot. She chewed on her bottom lip, then smiled. "What I'd *really* like," she announced boldly, "is the use of the house on St. Barts for a week . . . and *him*."

THREE WEEKS LATER she arrived on St. Barthélémy. Having woken up at four-thirty that morning to pack and catch the first plane out of JFK, she was tired. Wearing the wools that a frigid predawn February morning in New York had demanded, she was sweaty. Greeting the beauty of the Caribbean through hot, heavy eyes, she was miserable. To top it all, the taxi she'd taken from the airport had had a flat tire several hundred yards from the villa, and desperate to lay her head on a fresh, cool pillow, she'd taken her things and left the driver to deal with his jack and spare.

Toting a duffel bag over one arm and a bag of books and her purse over the other, she struggled along the narrow road, which wound uphill. Though she clung to its shoulder, where the succession of palm parasols might protect her from the strong midday Caribbean sun, she felt beads of sweat gather along her hairline, moisten her neck, trickle in a tiny stream down the valley between her breasts. For the moment the beauty of the island was lost on her. She simply wanted to lie down.

She sneezed once and sniffled as the road curved, then moaned aloud when the familiar structure with its red-tiled roof and white stucco walls emerged from its tropical camouflage. That was all the incentive she needed to quicken her step. Her legs felt like rubber, but she didn't care. Another two minutes and she'd be there, sprawled in her favorite room—in *everybody*'s favorite room—with the overhead fan gently cooling the air, the palm fronds dancing on the skylight overhead, the sea strutting its lush azure stuff beyond the open sliding doors, from the sparkling white sands of the beachfront to the far horizon.

Fairly running the last few steps, she shifted from one elbow to the other the heavy wool sweater she'd already stripped off and dug into her purse for the key. When it eluded her, she tugged the purse around and peered bleary-eyed into the scrambled abyss of its interior. She rummaged again, whispered a soft oath and peered a second time, finally shaking the bag to hear the telltale rattle that helped her zero in on the spot. Another minute's ferreting produced the key.

With a twist of her hand, the front door opened. As cool air enveloped her, she smiled her relief. "Thank you, Martine," she rasped softly, vowing to repeat it louder later in the week when she came face to face with the woman who must have been in earlier that morning in anticipation of her arrival. And a twist of fate it was that Martine was a morning person. Leslie's original plans had been to arrive that evening; only a last minute cancellation on the early-bird flight had brought her in at noontime.

Closing the door behind her, she stooped to let her bags fall from her damp and tired shoulders. Her purse and sweater slid to the floor nearby. Mopping her clammy forehead on her sleeve, she stepped out of her leather pumps and, with her fingers at the button of her plum-and-blue plaid skirt, started down the stairs.

After ten years of family vacations here, she'd come to take the villa for granted. Only a visitor would be entranced by its unique design. Nestled into the cliffs rising above the sands on the western end of the small island, it sprawled across three spacious levels. The top level, even with the road, held the front foyer, one wall of which was glassed and looked out toward the ocean, the other two walls of which opened to lateral bedrooms. The bottom level, to the right as the house followed the natural cropping of the cliff, held the airy kitchen and living room and opened on to a flagstoned terrace, itself graduated on two planes, the lowest of which was a hop, skip and jump from the beach.

It was the middle level of the house to which Leslie headed unswervingly. Connected to top and bottom by an open staircase, it was the one most coveted by whichever family member had the good fortune to arrive first, or, all too often and to Leslie's misfortune, needed the space. This level held an airy den and the exquisite master-bedroom suite, of which Leslie had every intention of taking sole possession for the week.

Bent on undressing and showering, she had her skirt unzipped and halfway down her hips by the time she reached the foot of the stairs. Quickly hopping free of the heavy wool, she tossed it over the back of a chair in the den, then reached down to pull her lavender turtleneck jersey from the elastic confines of her matching wool tights. Feeling more like a wilting violet than a stylish New Yorker, she padded toward the bedroom.

The door was open. Tugging the turtleneck over her head, she stumbled across the threshold, and was in the process of peeling the clinging fabric from her sweaty arms when she cried out in alarm and came to an abrupt halt. Clamping her teeth into her soft lower lip, she stared at the bed.

It was supposed to be empty. It was supposed to be freshly made and waiting just for her. It was supposed to be all hers for the week.

Instead, the covers were pulled back, and the rumpled sheets were draped—just barely—over a large body that was very definitely male and just as definitely sound asleep.

Sagging against the doorjamb with her turtleneck crushed against the pale mauve lace of her bra, she was seized by a wave of fury. Tony had promised! He'd said he would clear it with the others so that she might have the villa to herself for the week! Was this a friend of his? Or Diane's...or Brenda's? It just wasn't fair! The one time she'd wanted it...wanted it....

Suddenly her anger faded as a memory seemed to mesh with the tableau before her. Decorated in white and rattan, with pillows and cushions of an imported Italian weave, the room glowed beneath the noontime sun, which stole through the palms above the skylight to lend a dreamlike quality to the air. The ceiling fan whirred softly overhead, augmenting the gentlest of breezes that danced off the ocean and whispered in through the open glass sliding doors. But it was to the bed that Leslie's eyes were riveted. To the bed...and the figure so carelessly spread atop it.

There was something familiar about him. Feeling a sneeze coming on, she pressed her hand to her nose in hopes of suppressing it as, entranced, she studied the limp torso and sprawled limbs. The length of lightly bronzed leg that extended from the sheet spoke of superior height. The firmness of his thigh and corresponding leanness of his stomach attested to commendable fitness. The solidly muscular structure of his shoulder hinted at bodily pride. He was, in a word, stunning.

He lay on his back with his head fallen to the side. One hand, fingers splayed, rested on his stomach. She couldn't help but note how comfortable it looked, cushioned by the soft ribbon of hair that narrowed from the more ambitious covering of his chest. His other hand was thrown out to the side in a gesture she might have seen as pure invitation had the man not been so very obviously asleep.

Hugging her jersey to her throat, Leslie dared creep closer. Eyes wide in disbelief, she stared. She'd seen that face before. Even in repose it held a certain expression of vulnerability that immediately conjured up images of another bed, another setting. There was the hair, dark and mussed by sleep...the nose, straight, almost aristocratic...the sensually enticing shadow of a beard. As her eye tripped down his body once more, her heart began to pound with understanding. Oh, yes, she'd seen that face before. *And* that body. This time there was no workbench in the background, no sculptor's tools, no half-finished piece of art. This time his sheet covered the strip of flesh at his hip that had so taunted her before. This time the bed was in no photographer's studio but in her family's own villa.

Without realizing what she was doing, she sniffed the air in search of the unique scent of Homme Premier. But her nose was so stuffed she only succeeded in sending herself in a paroxysm of coughing, from which she emerged in horror to watch the man on the bed begin to move.

First his chest expanded with a deep, indrawn breath. His lips thinned, his brow furrowed. He turned his dark head on the pillow, stretching the outflung arm up over his head. Leslie swallowed hard when the sheet slipped precariously low on his abdomen.

Her gaze returned to his face in time to see one eye open—and stare at her blankly. When it was joined by the other, she saw that they were a warm shade of brown. The man blinked, dusting thick mahogany fringes against the high line of his cheek, then frowned, then blinked again and stared at her. Finally, as though abruptly recalling something, he bolted upright.

"My God!" he exclaimed, thrusting his fingers through the thick swath of hair that waved gently over his brow. "I'm sorry! I was going to be up and showered and dressed long before you arrived!" Frowning again, he looked toward the skylight, then reached for his watch from the stand beside the bed and stared at it in confusion. "Twelve-forty? But you weren't supposed to be in until seven tonight."

"I got an early flight," Leslie droned in a near monotone, then shook her blond head in distress. "I . . . don't . . . believe it."

"What don't you believe?"

"You."

His expression was immediately endearing, as though his only purpose in life was to please her, and having failed that, he was crushed. "I've done something wrong already?"

"You're here. I don't . . . believe it."

All vestige of drowsiness gone, the man looked down at his body innocently, before breaking into a gentle smile. "I am here."

"An understatement," she muttered beneath her breath, then watched him hoist himself up against the headboard. He seemed to dominate not only the bed but the entire room. In turn, Leslie's eyes held dismay. "He really did it."

Her reference was clear. "Your brother? Of course he did it. It sounds like he adores you. Most likely he'd have given you *anything* you'd asked."

"But...a man? *You?*" Her dismay was fast turning to mortification. "I was supposed to be here alone," she said in a very small voice. Above and beyond all the special things she had planned for herself, she suddenly realized that this man was not only gorgeous, but he was a male model who was *paid* to be pleasing to women. In this case he'd been paid by her brother, *her own brother*, to spend the week with her! Her cheeks felt hotter than ever.

Beneath the sheet, he bent one knee out to the side. Leslie eyed its vivid outline with something akin to anguish, breathing only a marginal sigh when he safely adjusted the sheet over his hips.

"Alone is no fun," he countered softly. His eyes dropped from her face to her chest, taking in the straps of her bra, the disarray of the jersey, which she clutched more fiercely than ever to her breasts, the slender expanse of purple wool running from her waist to her toes. She assumed she must look like a lavender elf; in truth, she felt more like the court jester.

Following his gaze and for the first time realizing her state of dress, Leslie took a step backward. "Alone can be lots of fun," she argued, recalling the plans she had to read, to sunbathe in the buff, to amble around the island to her heart's content with no thought of any other living soul, for a change. It simply wasn't fair, she mused, then slanted him an accusing glance. "You're in *my* bed, you know." She felt on the defense both physically and emotionally.

But her brief spurt of belligerence was feeble and reflected her growing torment. Not only was she appalled that her brother had taken seriously what she'd said purely tongue-in-cheek, but she felt sicker by the minute.

"I thought this was the master suite," came the deep rejoinder.

"It is. And this time round, *I'm* the master." So she'd been telling herself for the past few weeks; it had been part of the lure of spending her vacation at the villa in solitude.

The man on the bed arched a brow and skimmed her defensive pose. "You don't look terribly masterful right now. As a matter of fact—" his dark brows knit and he sat forward "—you don't look terribly well. Are you feeling all right?"

In no mood to be witty or subtle, Leslie simply shook her head. "I was up before dawn to get to JFK and had to wait forever sweltering on St. Martin to catch the island hopper here. I'm hot and sweaty and just want to get out of these things and into a cool shower. Besides that, I've got a splitting headache and one hell of a cold." She took a stuffy breath. "In short, I feel awful!"

When the man quickly pushed himself up from the bed, she shut her eyes. All too well she remembered the sliver of smooth flesh by his hip. She didn't think she could take that just now.

"You mean your normal voice isn't as nasal?" came the note of amusement not far from her ear. Simultaneously an arm circled her shoulder and propelled her forward.

Feeling perfectly stupid, she opened her eyes, careful to keep them straight ahead as the bathroom door neared. "No, it's not," she managed, struggling with the *n*'s.

"That's too bad," the man replied softly, teasingly. "It's sexy. Deep and . . . sultry. That's it. Sultry."

"Sultry, as in hot and humid. And sweaty." Sexy was the last thing she felt.

At the bathroom door he slipped a hand to her forehead. "And feverish. Wait here."

Sagging against the jamb, she closed her eyes. Then, hit by a wave of dizziness, she gave up even the idea of a cooling shower. Suddenly nothing mattered more than lying flat. Turning, she stumbled back to the bed. The thought that the man whose body had warmed its sheets moments before might have a god-awful social disease was totally irrelevant to the situation. Her legs simply wouldn't hold her any longer.

With a soft moan she curled on her side, then, forgetting her company, rolled onto her back, clutching her jersey to her stomach with one hand and throwing the other arm across her eyes. When, moments later, the same arm that had led her toward the bathroom lifted her to a half-seated position, she groaned.

"Let me rest," she whispered, but her protector had other ideas.

"First, aspirin," he said gently. "Are you taking anything else?" She shook her head and docilely swallowed the tablets, washing them down with the water he'd brought. "There." He took the glass from her and eased her back onto the bed. Then he reached for the waistband of her tights and began to shimmy them over her hips.

"What are you doing?" she cried in alarm and squirmed away. When she tried to sit up, though, a firm hand pressed her flat. For the effort she'd made, her only reward was the sight of the pale blue briefs that ringed his hips. With strong, knowing hands he proceeded to peel the tights to her toes and off.

"Better?"

By twenty degrees at least. "Oh, yes."

"Want a shower now?"

She shook her head and rolled to her side again, pulling one of the pillows against her for comfort. "Not yet. I think I'll just lie like this for a while."

"Then I'll shower. Where are your bags?"

Her eyes were closed, his voice distant. If the man wished to rob her, she couldn't stop him. Her total concentration was on finding relief from the aches and pains that seemed to have suddenly invaded her body. "Upstairs. . . ."

If she was aware of the pad of footsteps on the stairs going up, then down, she made no sign. Nor did she turn her head when the faint hum of an electric razor filled the air, or when the spray of the shower rang out, or when the rustle of clothes in a suitcase ended with the glide of smooth cotton over hair-roughened flesh. It was only when the aspirin began to take effect, when she felt just warm, rather than hot, when the pounding in her head had subsided to a dull throb, that she opened her eyes again.

Seated in a chair by the bed, wearing nothing but a pair of pleated khaki shorts, was the man she'd been given for her birthday. A rush of mortification hit her anew. For, sitting there, his hair and skin damp and fresh, his chest broad and manly, his shoulders strong and inviting, he looked more magnificent than he had in his ad. By contrast she felt as though she'd been dredged up from hell.

"I don't believe it!" she moaned, then felt all the more gauche when the faintest of smiles curved his lips.

Propping his elbows on the arms of the chair, he threaded his fingers together. "I think you've said that already."

"I don't care! This is incredible!"

"What is?"

"This. . . ." She waved toward him, then herself, then extended her fingers to take in the situation as a whole. "I can't believe Tony would do this to me!"

"As I was told, you specifically requested it."

Her chest rose and fell as she labored to breathe. "It was a *joke*! I was being facetious! Tony must have known that." When the man opposite her slowly shook his head, she went quickly on. "And besides, the man I pointed to was a fictitious character."

"He had a face and a body. You had to know he was real."

"He was a paid model! I never expected Tony to go out and track him down, then hire him to entertain me for the week!" The thought instantly revived her embarrassment. Pink-cheeked, she turned her face away and shut her eyes. "God," she moaned beneath her breath, "I feel so lousy. Maybe I'd be laughing if I felt all right. But I can barely breathe, let alone think straight."

The mattress yielded to another form. Though she tensed up, she didn't have the strength to move, even when a cool hand began to stroke damp strands of blond hair from her brow. Quite against her will, she found the gesture a comfort.

"How long have you felt this way?" the deep voice probed with such concern that she couldn't help but answer.

"Since last night."

"Sore throat?"

She shook her head, then opened her eyes and peered up into his, which were studying her carefully. "You can't stay here, you know."

"Oh?" The twinkle in his eye spoke of his amusement.

"No."

"And why not?"

"Because *I'm* here."

The man made ceremony of looking around the bed. "We seem to be doing just fine here together." Anticipating her, he had a hand at her shoulder before she could begin to raise it from the bed. "Besides, I'm your gift. You can't just discard me along with the wrapping."

"What wrapping?" she quipped. "Seems to me you weren't wearing much of anything."

"I was wearing something."

"Not much."

"So you *did* notice. I was beginning to think I'd lost my touch."

Leslie sighed and closed her eyes. "You haven't lost your touch," she granted. It was moving in slow circles against her temples. "Great for headaches. . . ."

"And . . .?"

Her eyes flew open. "That's all," she said quickly. "I meant what I said before. You can't. . . ." Her voice trailed off as a sneeze approached. "Damn," she whispered, covering her mouth and sneezing. She sat up in time to sneeze a second time, then took the tissue he offered and blew her nose. "Do I ever feel lousy. . . ."

The same hand that had smoothed her hair from her brow now tucked random strands behind her ear. "Why don't you take that shower? In the meantime, I'll fix you a cold drink."

"You can't stay. . . ."

"Have you had any lunch?"

"Lunch? I haven't had any *breakfast*. Feed a cold, starve a fever . . . I've got both. What do I do?" She raised her eyes to those above her. They were reassuring and confident.

"Don't worry, sweetheart. I know what to do. Here, you stay put." He pushed himself from the bed and reached for her bag. "What do you want to put on?" Unzipping the stylish duffel, he began rummaging inside. "Is there a nightgown in here?"

Leslie recalled the ad that had started this farce. Her voice held more than a trace of sarcasm. "Nightgown as in silky white negligee?" She shook her head. "Sorry."

For a minute the man raised his head and eyed her strangely. Then, as understanding dawned, he cast her a punishing glance and turned his attention back to her bag.

Perhaps it was her reference to the ad that did it. Perhaps it was simply the aspirin clearing her head. But in the moment's pause it occurred to Leslie that she was lying on a rumpled bed in nothing but scant wisps of mauve lace, watching a total stranger fish through her clothes.

"Here, let me do that," she said crossly as she pushed herself up. Within seconds she'd managed to extract the oversize T-shirt she'd come to think of as her Caribbean negligee. A very pale aqua from too many washings, it was likewise soft and comfortable. Easily reaching her thighs, it would be suitably unappealing. "If it's sexy you're looking for," she muttered, "you've come to the wrong place."

Mustering her pride, she snatched her bag of toiletries from the duffel and headed for the bathroom, totally unaware of how truly sexy she looked. The man watching her, however, was not. He stood holding the picture of her in his mind's eye long after the bathroom door had closed.

On the other side of the door, Leslie pressed her palms to her hot cheeks, then slid her fingers up to push her hair away from her face. A mess. She was a mess. The entire situation was a mess. How had she ever managed it . . . careful, conservative Leslie?

Angrily plopping the bag of toiletries atop the vanity, she dug inside for makeup remover. Makeup? Hah! What a wasted effort that had been. She'd looked deathly regardless. But New York was New York, and one didn't show one's face in public unless it was suitably protected from the elements. Lips thinning with sarcasm, she squeezed a gob of cold cream onto her fingers and began to scrub at her cheeks. Protected from the elements? More likely camouflaged. Hidden. Shielded from the world by a manufactured sheen. How phony it all was!

With a vengeance she tissued off the cold cream, then bent low to rinse her face with water. There she lin-

gered, savoring the sensation of coolness on her cheeks
and eyes. At last she straightened and pressed a towel
more gently to her skin.

She should have known... should have known never
to even joke with Tony about the state of her love life.
He'd been after her for years to marry, have an affair,
get involved, live it up. Wasn't that what he'd been doing since his own divorce six years before? Not that she
criticized him. He'd married young and had been faith-
ful to the letter to Laura. In the end she had been the one
to run off with someone else, leaving him to cope with
three growing children. He was a hardworking, devoted
father who needed time off once in a while; Leslie certainly couldn't fault him for his own choice of outlet.

On the other hand, she reasoned, as she turned on the
shower and stepped beneath its tepid spray, he should
have known not to foist something as... as prepos-
terous as this pretty boy on her! Hadn't she spent the
past ten years trying to show the world how different
she was? She'd had her fill of high society back in high
school. And in college, well, Joe Durand had soured her
on men, period. But then, Tony knew nothing about
Joe. She hadn't spoken of him to anyone. The self-
reproach with which she lived was bad enough, but to
air her folly for the sake of others' enjoyment... *that* she
didn't need.

Adjusting the water to a warmer temperature, she
shampooed her hair, then soaped herself. It was several
minutes later when she stepped from beneath the soothing spray. After toweling herself as vigorously as her
tired arms would allow, she drew on the T-shirt and a
fresh pair of panties and blew her hair nearly dry. Then,
standing opposite the misted mirror, she studied herself.
Even the mist couldn't soften the image.

"Pale, Leslie. Too pale," she announced, then sneezed
and reached for a piece of Kleenex. By the time she faced

herself again, the mist had begun to clear, and what she saw gave her a jolt. Oh, the features were fine—soft amethyst eyes that were large and, if anything, set a bit too far apart; a nose that was certainly small enough to balance the delicacy of her mouth and chin; hair that was an enviable shade of blond, cut into long bangs across the brow, trimmed crisply an inch above the shoulder, cropped stylishly at the sideburns and falling into place as Diego had promised. No, the features were fine, taken one by one. Put together, however, they formed the image of a lost and lonely waif.

Reaching up, she brushed her bangs from her eyes. What was she going to do? Granted, it was unfortunate that the one week she'd chosen to spend in the sun should be hampered by a mean winter cold. That, though, she could live with. And the sun, the warm weather, would be potent medicine.

But this man, this model...this very handsome model...was something else. Never in a million years would she have sought such a man on her own. Indeed, pausing to think of the man's occupation, of the many women he must have serviced over the years, she was appalled. And embarrassed. She wasn't that type at all! She wouldn't know what to *do* with such a man....

Shaking her head half in regret, she left the sanctuary of the bathroom to find the bedroom immaculate. The man's suitcase that had lain on the low glass table was gone, as were odds and ends atop the nightstand. The bed had been freshly made, its covers turned back invitingly. Padding barefoot to the walk-in closet, she peered inside, then turned. There was no sign of him.

While urging herself to simply climb into bed and be grateful she'd been left alone, Leslie headed downstairs toward the kitchen. He'd said he'd make her a cool drink. Well, she was thirsty.

Indeed he was in the kitchen, though his attention

was not on making a cool drink. Rather, he stood before the open window, his back to her, his arms crossed over his chest, one bare foot propped on the low rung of a nearby stool. He wore the same shorts he'd put on earlier, and all in all, he presented a perfect image of reflective masculinity.

For a lingering moment she studied him. Though his hair was thick and on the long side, it was well trimmed. From the sturdy nape to the soles of his feet, he looked clean. He also looked older than she'd imagined him to be, despite the prime condition of his body. From where she stood she caught shadings of silver following the gentle curve of each ear. Rather than detracting from his appearance, these silver streaks lent him an air of dignity that puzzled her all the more.

In short, there was nothing unsavory-looking about him. She wasn't sure what she'd expected from a gigolo. Certainly not . . . this.

With practically no warning she sneezed, ending her moment of invisibility. The man by the window turned quickly, his features instantly released from whatever thoughts had held them taut.

"There you are," he said, taking the few steps necessary to end their separation. "Feeling better?"

She had been, she'd thought. Now, though, looking up that great distance into a face that seemed so gentle, so knowing, she felt suddenly small and utterly insignificant.

"A little," she murmured, adding "self-conscious" to the list. What had made her think that a T-shirt would protect her from the eyes of a professional lover? When those eyes began to wander across her chest and down, she slithered from their touch and took refuge on the stool by the window.

"Why aren't you in bed?" he asked softly.

"I felt like seeing what you were up to," she answered

defensively, then turned her face to catch the ocean's gentle breath. "Where's that cool drink you promised?" Even to her own ears her tone held a touch of arrogance. It bothered her. She didn't much care for hired help.... certainly not of this sort!

After a pause came a murmured, "Coming right up." Only when Leslie heard the refrigerator door open did she dare look back to find her attendant on his haunches sorting through the packed shelves. "It looks like someone was far more prepared for your arrival than I was," he said, pushing aside a bushy head of lettuce to get at a carton of eggs. "I wouldn't have believed they had all this fresh produce down here."

"Some of it is home grown, but most of it's imported. And it was Martine who did the marketing. She's a marvel. She comes in to clean once or twice while we're here and keeps an eye on things when we're not. All it takes is one call from the States and the house is open, cool and stocked to the hilt."

"You don't ever rent it out."

"No. Friends use it sometimes. But more often it's just us." She tried desperately to be tactful. "We were very lucky to get this land. It's on a prime part of the island. Most of the space is owned by small inns. In fact, there's a quaint one just around the bend. You could probably get a room there...."

Ignoring her suggestion, he added a quart of milk and a package of neatly wrapped cheese to the growing assortment in his arms. "Nice cheese. Any lemon? Ah, there." When, arms laden, he stood at last, his knees cracked in protest. He flexed them gingerly as he deposited his armload on the counter.

Leslie focused in on the knees. "How old are you?"

"Thirty-nine."

"That old?" Even with creaking knees and the twin streaks of gray behind his ears, she would have given

him no more than thirty-five. "Aren't you a little...
beyond this type of thing?"

"Beyond cooking?"

"Beyond modeling. And...." She waved her arm in a
gesture to indicate his dubious role as her supposed
birthday present. "I always thought you had to be
younger...."

"To bring pleasure?"

"To do it...like this...." The heat on her cheeks
soared when he turned teasing eyes her way.

"Are you trying to say something, Leslie?"

"Yes," she declared in frustration, growing clammy
all over. "You can't stay here for the week! You've got
to leave; it's as simple as that!"

Reaching for a skillet, he put it on the stove, added a
dollop of butter and lit the gas. "While you're under the
weather? No way. As it is, I've got to redeem myself for
not being up and ready when you arrived."

She held up a hand. "No apologies. I'm sure someone
in your...field...is used to sleeping late." It had been
twelve-forty, for heaven's sake! She couldn't remember
the last time she'd slept that late herself. On second
thought, she could. It had been the summer before,
when she'd been hooked on *Noble House*. Not that
she'd loved it that much, but she made a practice of
never leaving a book midway through, and there had
been another book she'd been dying to start. "Late
nights and all...."

"And all."

"So—" she sent him an accusatory glance "—you've
found your way around the island? Gustavia has its
lively spots. When did you say you arrived?"

"Yesterday. And I haven't been anywhere but the airport and here. Actually, I was up late reading. I was in
the middle of a book I didn't really care for and I wanted
to start another, but I have this practice of never leaving

a book midway through, and it wasn't until five this morning that I finally finished it."

Leslie swallowed hard, sneezed again and put her palm to her head. Things weren't going as she'd planned. Not by a long shot.

"What are you doing?" she cried when she felt her feet leave the floor.

"Getting you back to bed. Don't worry. These weary old bones won't drop you."

"That's not the point."

"Then what is?" He took the stairs two at a time, carrying her as though she weighed no more than a small child.

The point? What *was* it, anyway? Her head was suddenly muddled again so badly that Leslie neither knew nor cared. When she felt the coolness of the sheets she breathed a sigh of relief and, curling onto her side, closed her eyes.

SHE MUST HAVE DOZED OFF. By the time she awoke, the face of the sun had shifted from the skylight overhead to the sliding doors, lower and farther west. Blinking away her grogginess, she followed its rays to the tall figure propped casually in the chair by her bed.

Deep in thought, he didn't see her at first. His legs were sprawled before him, his elbows bent on the cushioned arms of the chair, his hands fisted inside each other and pressed to his lips. She wondered what thoughts held him in his distant world, then shuddered when she realized how very far that world was from her own. The faint movement was enough to bring him back.

The slowest of smiles gentled his lips. "Hi, there."

"Hello."

Reaching to the stand beside him, he lifted two more pills and an ice-filled glass. Without a word, she swallowed the aspirin, washed it down with several gulps of what proved to be fresh lemonade, then drained the glass. When she leaned back, it was to rest against the pillows that he'd newly puffed.

"Not bad...the lemonade, that is." In truth, what she'd been thinking was how nice it was to have someone taking care of her for a change. A small luxury...a birthday gift. Her expression grew exquisitely soft. "When I was a child I loved Steiff pets—you know, those little stuffed animals—" she reached up and caught the upper part of her ear "—with the tiny tag right about here? They used to come with names attached to their ribbons." She moved her hand to the hollow of her throat, then, almost timidly, raised her eyes to his. "Do you have a name?"

For a heart-stopping moment, he held her gaze. She felt drawn to him, much as earlier she'd been drawn to the kitchen when she'd known she should have stayed in bed. He had power. It had touched her from the pages of *Man's Mode*. It had touched her when he'd stood at the kitchen window with his back to her. It had touched her moments before when his eyes had been distant. A kind of dreamlike quality. A depth. A puzzlement.

Slowly, with the corners of his eyes crinkling in a most effective way, he smiled. "Oliver Ames, at your service."

Oliver Ames. Her heart skipped a beat.

2

"OLIVER AMES." She said it aloud, testing it on her tongue. It flowed without any effort at all. Just right for a model—or a playboy. "Is that your...professional name?"

His mouth twitched at one corner. "Yes."

"And your real name," she asked more softly. "What's that? Or...is it off limits?" There were rules governing this sort of thing; unfortunately, she wasn't well versed in them.

Oliver smiled openly, his lips mirroring the dance of humor in his eyes. Sitting forward now, he was fully attentive.... *As rightly he should be,* Leslie mused. Wasn't he paid to be attentive? He was also paid to be attractive: bare chested, bare legged, large and vibrantly male—she found him disconcertingly so.

"No," he allowed lightly, "it's not off limits. As long as you don't spread it around."

"And who would I spread it to?" she snapped in response to the unsettling twist of her thoughts. "In case you haven't noticed, I'm not too...comfortable with this situation. Not much of a chance of my running back to Manhattan shouting the name of the guy my brother *bought* for me." She grimaced. "No woman wants to think she can't find someone on her own."

For an instant, when his dark brows knit, she feared that she'd offended him. Yet when he spoke, his voice held only curiosity.

"Can't you?"

"I'm not looking."

"And if you were? Surely there are men in New York who'd give their right arms for a Parish."

Leslie's lips grew taut, her expression grim. "If a man needed a Parish badly enough to sacrifice his right arm, I'd say he's sold himself short. And yes, there are many men like that around. Funny how money can screw up priorities." Closing her eyes, she slid lower on the pillows.

The creak of the rattan chair gave warning that Oliver Ames had moved. It wasn't until the bed dipped by her side, though, that she felt alarm. Eyes flying open, she found him settled near her hip, his arms propped on either side of her, hemming her in.

"You sound bitter," he observed. His voice was deep and kind and not at all taunting, as it might as have been, given the fact that it was a Parish who had dreamed up the very scheme that had brought him to St. Barts. "You've been hurt?"

She shrugged, unwilling to elaborate. For she couldn't think of the past when the man before her dominated the present. What was it about him, she asked herself, as she stared into eyes the texture of warm chocolate, that made her want to forget that he was what he was? What was it that made her want to reach up and brush the hair from his brow, trace the firm line of his lips, scale the gentle swell of his shoulder? What was it that stirred senses on which she'd long since given up? What was it that affected her so, that even now, as she lay in bed with a stuffy head and clenched fists, entranced her to the point of distraction?

"Your name," she whispered, then moistened her lips with her tongue. "Your real name. What is it?" Her expectant gaze fell to his lips and she waited, admiring the strong shape of them, until at last they moved to form the words.

"Oliver Ames," he mouthed, then gave a boyish grin.

"You're making fun of me," she contended soberly. "It was an innocent question."

"And an innocent answer. My name *is* Oliver Ames. Personal. Professional. Oliver Ames." He tipped his head to the side. "Perhaps you're the one doing the mocking. Is there something wrong with Oliver Ames?"

"Oh, no!" she breathed. "It's fine. It's more than fine. I like it. It's just that...well...it flows so easily I thought you'd made it up." She was babbling and she knew it. He seemed so close, his voice so deep and smooth that she felt rattled.

"My parents made it up. You can thank them one day."

Embarrassed, Leslie wrinkled her nose. "Oh, I couldn't do that...." Her voice trailed off. A lover for hire...and his parents? Great! Then she grew curious. "Do your parents...do they know what you do for a living?"

"Sure."

"And...they don't mind?"

"Why would they mind?"

She shrugged and fumbled. It didn't help that Oliver had moved his hands closer, that his thumbs had slyly found their way into her sleeves to ever so faintly caress the soft skin of her upper arms. "Oh, you know.... Modeling, and...this...." She waved one arm half in hopes of dislodging his hand. The gesture only seemed to solidify his grasp. And Oliver Ames was more amused than ever.

"Actually," he offered wide-eyed, "they're quite proud of me."

"Oh."

"Uh huh." He grinned. "A parent's love is all-abiding, wouldn't you say?"

She couldn't say much. A breathy, "I guess so," was

all his closeness would permit. Her gaze fell briefly to his chest, but the sight of the light furring of hair there was all the more unsettling, so she forced her attention back to his eyes. Her insides burned; much as she wanted to blame the sensation on the aspirin she'd taken, she couldn't.

"You'll catch my cold if you sit this close," she warned as she tried to sink more deeply into the bed.

"I don't mind," came the silky reply.

"But...then where would you be?" she persisted, unable to free herself from his sensual spell, struggling against its hold by voicing frantic wisps of thought. "I mean, who wants a red-nosed model with glassy eyes? Who wants a lover with a stuffed nose and the sneezes? As it is there are already too many communicable diseases rampant in your trade—"

"Ah, so that's what frightens you—catching something from *me*?"

"I'm not frightened."

"Then why are you trembling?"

"Because...I'm sick."

To her chagrin he moved one hand to her forehead "You feel cooler. You're not even as pale. No, there must be something else that's given you the shakes."

"I don't have the shakes!" she declared loudly, then clamped her mouth shut when even her voice belied her claim. It was sheer chemistry. She knew it, and it mortified her. Granted, he was a pro. But to be so totally susceptible to him appalled her. "And if I do, it's your fault. You're the one who's making me nervous. Damn it, you should be some kind of arrogant, unsavory creep, with little bugs crawling around here and there."

"I'm not," he stated, his voice calm. "And there aren't any bugs."

"I know," she replied miserably. It was obvious that the man was both clean and healthy. She didn't have to

ask; she just knew. Besides, she trusted Tony. Though
his sense of humor was sadly misguided, he did love
her. And he was protective. Hadn't she kept her experience with Joe Durand from him partly out of fear of
what he might do to Joe? No, Tony would never have
invited anyone objectionable to spend the week alone in
a villa with his little sister. Tony would have checked
everything out. Strange. A male model checking out? A
paid escort? In *Tony's* book?

"Well . . . ?" Oliver asked softly, his face no more than
a hand's width from hers.

"Well what?" she managed to whisper.

"The verdict. I can see those little wheels going round
and round in your head. Will you let me kiss you . . . or
am I going to have to be forceful about it?"

"Forceful? Truly?" she asked softly.

His forearms came to rest flush on the sheet, bringing
his abdomen into contact with hers. Leslie caught her
breath, aware of his warmth and of the precious nothings
she wore beneath her shirt. Meanwhile, hidden high up
her sleeves, his fingers cupped her shoulders and gently
massaged their tautness. Her response, an instinctive coil
of heat that sizzled its way to her toes and back, made
moot the point. He would never use force. He wouldn't
have to. He was good, she mused in dismay. Too good.

"Don't . . ." she heard herself say, then looked as
puzzled as he.

"Don't what? Don't touch you? Don't kiss you? Don't
take care of you?"

She wanted . . . she didn't. "Just don't . . . ."

"But I have to," he whispered.

Her voice was no louder, though tinged with regret.
"Because you were hired?" The word stuck in her throat
like a large piece of overcooked liver. She swallowed
hard to dislodge it, managing to produce only a tiny
moan. He'd been hired to love her . . . and it hurt.

When he slid his fingers to the back of her neck and pressed feathery circles in her skin, she closed her eyes and turned her face away. "What is it?" he murmured. She simply shook her head and squeezed her eyes tighter. "Come on, Les," he coaxed. "Tell me." His thumb slid across her cheek to stroke the taut line of her jaw.

"This is...humiliating...."

"Why?"

"Because Tony...arranged for you," she said, feeling ugly and sick and sexless.

"And if I said that that had no bearing on this moment...?"

"I'd wonder whether it, too, wasn't part of the act." Very cautiously she opened her eyes to find Oliver studying her intently. Then, easing up, he clicked his tongue against the roof of his mouth.

"So distrustful...and at such a young age."

"I feel about twelve. And, yes, I'm distrustful. I...I guess I just want more out of life than the buying and selling of favors."

He thought for a minute. "What if you thought of this as a fix-up? Haven't you ever had a blind date?"

"Oh, yes." Her lips twisted. "Charming invention, the blind date."

"It has been known to work."

"Not in my book."

"And why not?"

"Because a blind date is never really blind. I mean, the person who agrees to a blind date usually does so at the convincing of a salesman in the guise of a matchmaker." When Oliver frowned she grew insistent. "Really." She stared at the ceiling and spoke in a mocking tone. "He's in his late thirties, is tall, dark and handsome, is a stockbroker, drives a Porsche and has a horse farm in upstate New York."

Oliver nodded. "Sounds interesting."

"Sounds vile! Who gives a damn if he's tall, dark and handsome, and has enough money to put DuPont to shame? I certainly don't! And I dislike the thought that I've in turn been marketed, based on similarly meaningless data."

"Ah . . . the Parish curse."

"Among other things," she mused, then took a breath and, emboldened by indignation, faced her tormentor. "So, Oliver Ames, if you want to kiss me, do so knowing that I earn my own living as a preschool teacher, that I drive a four-year-old VW Rabbit, that I hate parties, love picnics and abide by intrusions into my privacy only with great reluctance." Energy waning, she lowered her voice. "Also know that I'm very conservative. I don't sleep around."

He pressed his lips together, stifling a grin. "Then I don't have to fear catching something from you?"

"Yes. A cold."

"Which I'll risk. . . ."

Certain her diatribe would have discouraged him, Leslie was taken by surprise. She tried to tell herself who he was, *what* he was, but the fact of his presence muddled her brain. He was so near, so vibrant. When his head lowered, she closed her eyes. Her breath came faster; she heard its rasping. Surely that would put him off . . . but no. His lips touched her left eye first, whispering a kiss on its lid once, then a second time before inching away. The bridge of her nose received similar treatment, then her right eye and its adjoining temple.

What astonished her most was the reassurance she felt from his touch. It was light and gentle, imbuing her with an unexpected sense of contentment. From her temple it fell to her cheekbone, dotting that sculpted line with a string of feather kisses before moving on to savor the delicate curve of her ear. The warmth of his breath made her tingle. Unknowingly she tipped her head to the side to ease his access.

"Nice?" he whispered against the high point of her jaw.

"Mmmmmmm."

"Relaxing?"

"Very."

"I'm glad," he murmured against her skin as he nibbled his way along her jaw, giving special attention to the delicacy of her chin before raising his head.

In a daze of pleasure, Leslie opened her eyes to find Oliver's, warm and alive, trained on her lips. His touch was a tangible thing, in the name of seduction doing something destructive to relaxation.

"I shouldn't let you . . ." she whispered meekly.

"But you can't help yourself . . . any more than I can," he answered, moments before he lowered his head and touched his lips to hers.

She stiffened at first, struck by the utter intimacy of the act. Only a kiss . . . yet it probed her entire being. Though his lips were gentle, they slid over hers with expertise—lightly at first, sampling, tasting, then with greater conviction as he sought her essence.

"Relax, Les," he whispered. "It's all right." His hands emerged from her sleeves to caress her shoulders from without.

"No . . . don't . . . ." It felt too good. She didn't trust herself.

Again he raised his head, and she met his gaze. His eyes were more smoky this time; she badly wanted to believe that she'd excited him.

"Kiss me," he said in a shaky breath, his eyes on her lips, then sliding upward. "Kiss me, and then decide." When she shook her head, he took a different tack, dropping his gaze to his hands, which glided up her shoulder to her neck, then inched downward from the hollow of her throat, downward over her chest, downward to separate over the straining fullness of her breasts.

Unable to push him away, unable to invite his advances, Leslie bit her lip to keep from crying out. Her eyes begged that he free her from the prison of his spell, yet her breasts swelled toward his touch in primal betrayal. His fingers circled her, working systematically inward, coming at last to the turgid peaks that spoke so eloquently of her arousal.

In self-defense she grasped his wrists and put a halt to the torture by pressing his hands hard against her. "Oliver, please don't."

"Will you kiss me?"

"I don't want to."

"You might like it."

"That's what worries me!"

Silence hung in the air, made heavy by the honesty of her argument. Frowning, Oliver studied her as though she was a creature like no other he'd ever known. In turn, she pleaded silently. She was sick . . . and aroused. It was a disturbing duo.

"You have the eyes of a fawn," he said at last. "Has anyone ever told you that?"

The spell was broken. With a shy smile of relief, she shook her head. "No."

"Well, you do." He sat straighter. "The eyes of a fawn. I could never hurt a fawn. So free and alive, so soft and vulnerable."

"You must be a poet. Funny, I thought you were supposed to be a sculptor."

"All illusion," he breathed magnanimously as he pushed himself off the bed. Only then did Leslie see what she wanted to. Very subtly and from the corner of her eye she saw sign of his arousal. Illusion? Not that. It was a heady thought on which to roll over and go to sleep.

SHE SLEPT through the late afternoon and early evening, awakening only to eat the light omelet Oliver had fixed, to take the aspirin he supplied, to drink the juice he'd chilled. She felt lazy and pampered and stuffy enough neither to object to the attention nor to raise the issue of his leaving the villa again. There would be time aplenty to discuss the latter when she felt better. For the time being, having a caretaker was rather nice.

Not used to sleeping at such length, she awakened periodically throughout the night. Each time, Oliver was in his chair by her bed, either sitting quietly, reading, or, at last, dozing. Though she might have enjoyed the luxury of watching him sleep, her slightest movement roused him every time.

"How do you feel?" he asked softly, leaning forward to touch the back of his hand to her brow.

"Okay."

"Any better?"

"I think so."

"Want a drink?"

"I just had one."

"That was two hours ago. Another would do you good," he argued, bounding from his chair to return to the kitchen for juice. In his absence, Leslie marveled not only at the image of his moonlit torso edged in silver, but at the easy intimacy of their soft-spoken conversation. To her astonishment there was something warm and reassuring about it.

Then he was back, standing guard while she drained the entire glass.

"I'll float away pretty soon."

"I'm your anchor. You won't get far. Now, be a good girl and go back to sleep."

"Hmmph. 'Be a good girl.' Lucky for you I'm the docile type. What would you have done if you'd had a wildcat on your hands?"

"I guess I'd have had to tie her hand and foot to the bed. Are you going to go to sleep?"

"In a minute. What time is it?"

"Two-twenty."

"Aren't *you* going to bed?"

"Is that an invitation?"

"Uh uh. Just a touch of concern. After all, if you let yourself get run down, you'll catch this cold but good!"

"Hey . . . which one of us is the doctor here?"

"Funny, I didn't think we had one."

"Oh, we have one, and it's me! Now go to sleep."

"I'm not tired."

"Not tired? You've got to be tired. You're sick."

"But I've been sleeping for hours." She started up from the bed. "What I really feel like doing is taking a walk on the beach."

Just as quickly, her shoulders were pressed flat. "No way, sweetheart. The bathroom is about your limit tonight."

"Come on. It's no fun walking around the bathroom. No sand, no shells, no waves—"

"Right! That gives you great incentive to get well."

"Really, Dr. Ames. I'm *not* tired."

He paused then. Even in the dark she felt the brand of his gaze. When, puzzled, she raised her head, she saw him push himself from his chair and approach the tape deck.

"Then we'll have some music. What'll it be?"

Sighing her resignation, she laid her head back. "You choose." Then, recalling his occupation and suddenly fearing that his choice might be something loud and swinging, she wavered. "On second thought—"

"Too late. My choice it is."

Moments later the soft and gentle strains of Debussy wafted into the air. Leslie lasted for all of five minutes before she fell back to sleep.

WHEN SHE AWOKE it was dawn. Pale purples and blues lit the sky, filling the room with their opalescent hues. She was alone. Alone and unguarded. Quickly shaking off the last traces of sleep, she put her feet on the floor and stood up. Cold or no cold, she'd had her fill of bed. This was her vacation. Oliver Ames could do something quite pithy with his orders, *she* was going to the beach.

Walking stealthily, half expecting her keeper to pop up from around the corner and usher her back to bed, she left the bedroom. Finding the den empty she headed for the stairs, tiptoeing down their bleached wood planks and pausing on the lowest rung. Still no sign of him. The kitchen was empty. The tile felt cool beneath her bare feet as she sped toward the glass sliding doors. When she flipped back the lock, its echo made her wince. Looking cautiously behind her, she waited. Still nothing. Dallying no longer, she quietly slid the door open and stepped out onto the terrace.

A long, deep breath told her that her cold was better. For the first time since she'd arrived, she smelled the special aroma of the island. Fresh in the morning's first light, it was a blend of sand and salt and lush tropical verdancy, a bouquet evoking lavish thoughts of laziness and leisure.

With a smile, she crossed beneath the palms of the terrace, trotted down the few stairs to the lower level, paused once again to savor the setting, then took the last set of steps at a clip. Ahh, to be finally on the beach!

Her smile spread into a full-scale beam. There was nothing like it! She wiggled her toes in the superfine sand, squished forward several steps, wiggled her toes some more, then sat down. It was beautiful as always, the beach, the sea. Her lungs drank it in, her eyes devoured it. Every one of her senses opened greedily.

Sitting cross-legged with the cushion of sand conforming to the lines of her bottom, her thighs, her calves, she thrust her fingers into the fine white stuff, heedless of the grains catching beneath her nails, simply eager to feel it all close up. Her eyes tripped forward over the softest of sand to that damp area where the surf had recently played. Here and there small shells winked, half buried in the tawny beach. And beyond was the restful ribbon of the tide, swishing this way and that with each incoming wave, rhythmic and gentle and positively addictive.

Stretching her legs forward, Leslie dropped back onto her elbows. Facing west as she was, the sunrise was behind her. Yet far ahead across the turquoise depths, discernible to none but the most watchful eye, were the faintest pink reflections of the morning sky.

She was glad she'd come. She needed this—this sense of the warm, the familiar, the relaxing. She'd always been able to think here, to walk off on her own or sit on the beach and put things into perspective. She needed that now. She'd been troubled of late. Where was she going? What did she want in life? Oh, yes, the preschool thrived, and indeed she loved her work. But something was lacking . . . something with which she had to come to terms.

On impulse she swiveled around on the sand until she faced the villa. Arms now straight behind, supporting her, she studied the sprawling house set into the rocks. Where was he? Surely he hadn't given up so easily and left in the predawn hours to find a more hospitable welcome in town. No, chances were he had simply made use of one of the bedrooms on the upper floor.

Her gaze rose to that level, slipping from one to the other of the large glass panes that marked each of the bedrooms in turn. Was he sleeping? Sprawled out in bed as he'd been when she'd first arrived? Wearing nothing but the bedsheet . . . and his Homme Premier cologne? Today she'd be able to smell it. Would it be musky? Tart? Woodsy? Spicy?

What was she going to do about him? Her plans hadn't included a live-in companion, particularly one as tall and good-looking as Oliver Ames. The mere mention of his name set small butterflies aflutter in her stomach. She'd wanted to spend her time here in total relaxation, letting it all hang out, so to speak. Yet, sexy as sin, Oliver Ames intimidated her. What was she going to do about him?

Whirling around again in frustration, she hugged her knees to her chest. Moments later she scrambled to her feet and began to walk slowly, pensively, along the water line. The soles of her feet slapped the wet sand; distractedly she eyed the pattern of granules dislodged from beneath her toes. Bending, she lifted a tiny mollusk shell, studied its spiral design, tossed it lightly back into the surf. Then she turned to face the ocean head-on, wishing she could find something, *anything* offensive about Oliver Ames. To her chagrin, there was only one thing—his occupation. A paid smile. A manufactured daydream. Prepackaged virility. And, oh yes, bedroom eyes. No doubt he was good at his job.

Perturbed, she returned to the powdery sand of the beach, stretched out with her hands layered beneath her head and closed her eyes. The sky was brightening steadily; the sun wasn't far behind. A tan. That was one of the things she wanted this week. A soft, even tan. All over.

Oliver Ames would have to leave! He'd just have to! How could she possibly lie nude in the sun with him around? Smiling, she recalled the first time she'd gone topless on a beach. It had been the year before they'd had the villa built, when she and her father and Tony and Laura and Brenda and John had flown down here to scout around. She'd been eighteen at the time, confident of her youth, if not her future. In no time she'd discovered that on the beaches of St. Barts one was more conspicuous with a bikini top than without. In no time she'd discovered the delightful intimacy of the sun's warm touch on her breasts. And the rest, oh, she'd discovered that several years later, on the only other occasion she'd chanced to be alone at the villa. She'd felt free and uninhibited and sensual then. It had been wonderful. . . .

Opening her eyes a smidgen, she squinted toward the rooftop of the house. Another hour and the sun would scale it. Would he be sleeping still? Closing her eyes again, she pictured *him* bathing nude in the sun. Long limbs connected by sinewed bonds, tautly drawn skin, swells here, indentations there, a mat of hair extending in varied patterns from chest to ankle. . . .

Sharply sucking in her breath, she sat upright. Eyes wide, she dug her teeth into her knee, welcoming the pain. Then, when the slightest movement caught her eye, she lifted her gaze to the villa.

He was there, standing at the window of her room, hands on his hips, his dark head moving slowly from side to side. She stared for a minute, then hugged her knees tighter and lowered her head again. She could almost hear it. *What are you doing out of bed? And on the beach before sunup? If it's pneumonia you're looking for, you're on the right track!*

Hearing the patter of his feet on the planking connecting the terrace levels, she stood quickly, propped her hands on her hips and adopted her most belligerent stance. "I don't care what you say, Oliver Ames," she called to the fast-approaching figure, "but I'm here! And I'm fine! And I have every intention of making the best of my vacation!" She paused only for a breath as Oliver's long legs carried him toward her. "Now—" she held up a hand "—I do appreciate what you did for me last night, but I'm fine. Really fine. So you don't need to feel any further responsibility—"

The breath was knocked out of her when Oliver took her firmly in his arms. His eyes glowed, his body pulsed. "Damn it, but you look sexy," he growled, then took her lips in a kiss so masterfully gentle it shattered all pretense of fight. "Good morning," he whispered against her mouth seconds later. "Sleep well?"

Leslie stared at him in shock. "Good morning?" she echoed blankly, then watched him eye the sky in amusement.

"It is morning, I believe. And a beautiful one at that." His arms remained around her waist, holding her lower body snug against his.

"But...what are *you* doing up at this hour? I was sure you'd be out 'til noon. I mean, you didn't get to bed until after two-thirty."

"Actually it was closer to three-thirty. But I like getting up early. Morning's the best time."

Was it the velvet softness of his voice or the glimmer in his eye that lent deeper meaning to his words? She didn't know. She didn't want to find out. Coward that she was, she put light pressure on his arms. When he released her instantly, she was only momentarily relieved. When without another word he took off at a trot toward the water, she felt disappointed. When he splashed in to thigh level, then dived forward in a graceful arc and began to swim away from shore, she felt abandoned.

Lips on the verge of a pout, she sank down on the sand and watched the dark head turn rhythmically with each stroke. He was a good swimmer. *But why not*, she asked herself. Men of his ilk were bound to have access to villas such as these, or estates with pools. Indeed, part of his appeal would be the slickness of his limbs as they propelled him smoothly through the waves. Even now he was probably wondering whether she was watching. Perversely, she twisted sideways on the sand

and studied the nearby palm. Tall and sturdy, graceful in a majestic kind of way, powerful, dignified, protective. . . . With a soft moan, she turned back to the sea.

Moments later Oliver emerged from the waves, his body wet and gleaming in the early morning light. Pulse racing, Leslie watched him approach.

"That was nice," he said breathlessly, rubbing a hand across his chest. Then, ducking behind her, he dragged a pad cushion from one of the lounge chairs tucked beneath the rocks and, returning to her side, spread the cushion flat. Within moments he lay on his back, his eyes closed, his hands folded on his stomach.

Unable to help herself, Leslie stared. Fit, indeed. His body was beautiful. Not perfect, mind you—there was a mole on his left shoulder, a tiny scar beneath his ribs. The gift of a jealous husband, perhaps? Or a scorned mistress?

Another scar caught her eye, this one slashing ever so slightly above the band of the slim-fitting trunks he wore. A low blow from a dissatisfied client?

"Appendectomy," came the timely explanation.

When Leslie's gaze shot upward, it caught Oliver's knowing smile. "I was wondering," she said hotly, "whether it was a battle scar."

He tucked in his chin to study his body. "This one is," he said, touching a finger to the small mark beneath the ribs. Then he moved the finger lower, following into his trunks and out again the faint ridge of the more daring scar. "This one's still pretty pink. I would have thought it should have faded more by now."

"When was it done?"

"Last winter." He put his head back down, closed his eyes again and gave a soft chuckle. "I'm not the best of patients. It was as much of a trial for the hospital as it was for me."

Somehow she couldn't believe it. Turning her head to

the side, she eyed him askance. "You mean to say that the nurses didn't appreciate your presence?"

"Not by a long shot. I suppose I wasn't very cooperative, but after two days of being pushed and pulled, rolled and prodded, undressed and bathed and powdered, I'd had it!" He inhaled a deep breath through his nose. "I guess I'm just not meant to be pampered."

A shame, she mused, since he seemed the perfect subject. Lucky nurses, to have free access to that body. . . .

She cleared her throat. "So you prefer to do the pampering, do you? I suppose . . . if the reward's great enough . . . ." She took a breath, then shut her mouth and slowly exhaled through her nose.

Oliver opened one eye. "What were you going to say?"

"Nothing."

"Do you gulp air often?" he teased gently.

"Only when it's preferable to putting my foot in my mouth."

"Come on. You can say anything to me." When she simply turned her head and studied the waves, he reached out to slide his fingers around her wrist. "Come on, Leslie . . . anything."

"Actually," she began timidly, "I was just wondering why you do it."

"Why I do what?"

"Model. Rent yourself out. I would think you'd want something a little more . . . more lasting."

"You don't approve of my . . . avocation?"

Avocation. On the nose. Part-time hobby or source of amusement. "Perhaps I don't understand it. I guess I'm more attuned to occupations. You know, full-time career types of things."

"As in preschool teaching?"

"Uh huh."

"But what about fun?" he asked, suddenly up on an

elbow looking at her. "You must have outside interests. There must be things you do on a lark."

"Is that what this is to you . . . a lark?"

For the first time there was a hint of impatience in his voice. "It's far more than that, Leslie, and you know it."

Of course. Tony had hired him. "Listen," she began, looking evasively at her toes, "this whole situation is extremely awkward. I appreciate Tony's thought in sending you down here, but now that we've had our laughs you can go on back to New York."

"I can't do that."

"Why not?"

"Because we haven't had our laughs. You stumbled in here sick as a dog yesterday. All I've had a chance to do is force liquid down your throat. Tony wouldn't be pleased."

"Tony doesn't have to know. You can go quietly back to New York, and I can tell Tony what a wonderful time we had. He'll never be any the wiser."

"And what about me? I've been looking forward to ten full days in the sun."

"Then I'll make a call and get you a room down the road."

"I don't want a room down the road."

"Don't you see," she exclaimed, growing more frustrated by the minute, "you can't stay here!"

For a minute he was quiet. His eyes roved her face, returning time and again to her eyes. "What are you afraid of, Leslie?" he asked at last. "There's got to be something hanging you up."

"There's nothing," she said quietly, all the while thinking how soft and coaxing his voice was.

"Look at me and tell me that."

She kept her eyes glued to the horizon. "There's nothing."

"Look at me," he whispered, his fingers tightening

almost imperceptibly around her wrist. When still she didn't comply, he gave a gentle tug. Catching her off balance, he pulled her down onto the sand. Before she could begin to recover, he'd pinned her down. "Now," he murmured, his eyes an ardent brown, "look at me and tell me what's on your mind."

"You!" she cried. "You! You shouldn't be here, Oliver Ames! You're all wrong for me! I need...I need...." Her voice trailed off, caught in her throat as the damp warmth of his body seeped through to her. "I need..." she whispered, mesmerized by the low glimmer of his gaze.

"I know what you need," Oliver whispered in turn, lowering his lips to her neck. "You need a man's loving." He pressed his mouth to her throat as she gave a convulsive swallow, then ran his tongue along an imaginary line to her chin. When he lifted his head to meet her gaze once more, he moved his body over hers. "You need me...."

3

HE WAS RIGHT in a way, she was later to muse. She *did* need a man's loving. But not just in the physical sense Oliver offered. She needed something deeper. A relationship—that was what was missing from her life. That was what she'd read in the ad. That was what she'd wanted when she had fingered Oliver's picture in response to Tony's magnanimous offer. She wanted love. A man, family, a home. And Oliver Ames, whose body was his prime negotiable commodity, was not the one to give it! Oh, yes, she found him attractive. Her body responded to him in precisely the way he intended. But there was far more to love than desire alone. Blinded by passion, she had made a fool of herself once. Never again.

"You need me," Oliver repeated in a husky whisper.

Leslie shook her head, her eyes awash with apprehension. "No. That's not true," she gasped, fighting his pull with every bit of determination she could muster.

Threading his fingers through hers, Oliver anchored her hands to the sand on either side of her head. "It is," he insisted. "Don't you see it? Don't you *feel* it?"

What she felt was the boldness of his body, hard and warm and aggressive, imprinting its maleness onto her. What she felt was the answering tremor of her limbs, the gathering of a heat deep within, the stoking of unbidden fires.

"I feel it," she cried softly, "but I can't, Oliver, I can't give in to it. Don't you see?" Her fingers clutched tightly at his, her eyes held a hint of desperation. "I can't view it the way you do. You may be able to jump from relationship to relationship, but I can't. I suppose I'm an anachronism in this day and age. But that's the way I am." Her voice lowered to a mere quaver. "I'm sorry."

With a harsh chuckle, Oliver rolled off her and sat up to stare at the sea. "Don't be sorry. It's really very... lovely."

Leslie watched the muscles of his back flex with a tenseness echoed by his jaw. Without a doubt, she'd made her point. What must he think of her now? Drawing in an unsteady breath, she sat up, then rolled to her knees. On a whim, wishing only to soften her dictate, she reached out to touch him, then thought twice and let her hand waver in the air before dropping it to her side. She'd wanted him to leave; now she'd simply given him further incentive.

Pushing herself from the sand, she headed for the stairs.

"Leslie?"

She paused, head down, her bare foot on the lowest rung. *Move, Leslie, move. Show him your grit. Show him you really don't care.* But she couldn't. Because she did care. Dubious life-style or no, she couldn't help but feel something for Oliver Ames.

"Leslie?" His voice was directly behind her now. She turned and looked up, then felt her insides flip-flop. His expression—so vulnerable, so very like that he'd worn in the ad.... But it couldn't be an act; there was something far too deep and needy.... "Listen, Les, I've got a proposition."

"Proposition?" *Oh, God, what now? He's imposing and appealing and powerful. A woman can only withstand so much....*

At her look of fear, his gaze gentled all the more. "Nothing compromising," he soothed, his lips curving into the ghost of a smile. "Just practical." When she stood her ground, he went on. "This is your vacation. The week was to be something special for you." He lifted a hand to her shoulder, wavered, dropped it. She couldn't help but recall her own similarly thwarted gesture moments before. "What say we call a truce? You go your way, I'll go mine. You take the master suite, I'll take the bedroom I used last night. I'd like to explore the island, so I'll stay out of your hair. You can do anything you'd intended to do all by yourself...unless you change your mind. If that happens—" his gaze dropped to her lips "—I'll be here."

Leslie studied him, trying to equate what he was with what he proposed. "You're apt to be very bored," she warned.

He laughed gently. "I doubt that." He cast a glance behind him. "With all this—and a good book, and a kitchen at my disposal—how could I be bored?"

She wondered what the kitchen had to do with anything. There wasn't a spare ounce of fat on the man, so he couldn't be that much of a glutton. "I can't promise you anything...."

"I'm not asking for promises."

"But...why? Why would you rather spend a quiet and uneventful week here than go to one of the resorts? I mean, I'm sure there'd be lots of women...."

At Oliver's punishing glance, she shut her mouth. "I don't want lots of women. Or action. You may not believe it, but quiet and uneventful *do* sound perfect to me." He thrust long fingers through his hair, only to have the damp swath fall right back over his forehead. Leslie was grateful that something else dared defy him, and grew bolder.

"You're right. I don't believe it," she quipped lightly. "I'm sure your life is an endless whirlwind of pleasure back in New York."

He grew more serious. "Pleasure? Not always. Sometimes the whirlwind seems more like a tempest. Which is one of the reasons I jumped at the opportunity to come down here. I need the break, Leslie. I'm tired." Indeed, she heard it in his voice at that moment. "Maybe you're right. Maybe I am getting too old for this kind of—" a glint of humor returned to his eye "—rootless existence. Maybe a week of . . . abstinence will do me good. Build my character, so to speak. Reform me. Set me on the straight and narrow."

"Fat chance," she muttered, but her resistance was token. True, she'd hoped to have the villa all to herself. True, his presence would keep her on her guard. But there was something quite . . . appealing about him. If she had to share the villa, she could have done far worse.

"What do you say?" he prodded in earnest.

"What *can* I say? After your talk of character building, I'd feel like a heel to refuse." Her eyes narrowed. "You were counting on that, weren't you?" He simply shrugged and broke away to start up the steps. "Where are you going?" she called.

On the terrace and fast receding, he yelled back, "I'm disappearing. As promised." Sure enough, within seconds he'd been swallowed up by the house.

Smiling, Leslie followed as far as the lower terrace, where she sank into one of the deck chairs to track the progress of a fishing boat as it returned to Gustavia with its early-morning catch.

An hour later her nose twitched, rousing her from her peaceful contemplation of the beauty of the sea. At first she thought she was about to sneeze, then realized that the awareness was of something quite different. Lifting her head, she sniffed the air, then she stood up and moved hesitantly toward the steps. Curious, she climbed them. Stomach growling, she crossed the upper tier of the terrace. Only when she pushed back the screen and stepped onto the inner tile did she have her first glimmer of understanding of Oliver's attraction to the kitchen.

"What have you *made*?" she asked, mouth watering, eyes wide and hungrily homing in on the kitchen counter.

Oliver sat at the table, deeply immersed in a book. Before him was a plate containing the swirling remnants of some maple syrup. "Belgian waffles," he said without looking up. "There are two left. Help yourself."

Sure enough, on a plate covered by foil were two plump, warm waffles. In nearby dishes were strawberries, confectionery sugar, maple syrup and whipped cream. She felt as though she'd been treated to a breakfast buffet brought in from one of the local resorts. Had it not been for the waffle iron, well scrubbed and dripping dry beside the sink, she might have suspected he'd done just that.

His empty plate settled into the sink. "When you're done," he murmured near her ear, "just leave everything. I'll be in later to clean up." She looked up in time to see him turn. The next thing she knew, she was alone.

She hesitated for only a minute before reaching for a clean plate and helping herself to the feast he'd prepared. It was delicious. But then, she'd been starved. What had she had yesterday—one light omelet and twenty glasses of juice? Surely she was on the mend, what with this newfound appetite.

Without a second thought, she cleaned everything when she'd finished, then climbed the stairs to ferret a bathing suit from her bag. Though there was no sign of Oliver, she wasn't taking any chances. Her suit was one piece—albeit cut out in back with a bevy of crisscrossing straps—and appropriately demure. Satisfied that her appearance would preclude invitation, she armed herself with a bottle of suntan lotion and a towel and headed for the beach.

The day was utterly restful. She sunned for a while, returned to the kitchen for a cold drink and her book, then spent several hours back on the beach in a lounge chair, reading beneath the shade of the waving palm, even dozing to the gentle swish of the waves. In response to the sun, the warmth and the rest, her cold continued to improve. She felt stronger by the hour and more encouraged. For true to his word, Oliver had gone his own way. Or so she assumed, since she saw neither hide nor hair of him. She felt relaxed and free, almost as though she had the villa to herself.

She didn't see him again that day. When she finally left the beach at afternoon's end, she found a large brown bag and a note on the kitchen table.

"Dinner," it read, "if you're in the mood. I've taken the bike and gone exploring. Hear the sunset is spectacular from Castelets. If I'm not back by dawn, I bequeath you my bag of books. Particularly enjoyed...."

Tuning out, she lifted her eyes in dismay. The motorbike. Of course, she wouldn't be able to hear it from the beach. But...to Castelets? Steep and jagged, the approaching drive had turned back many a cabbie in its day! So, she scowled and crushed the note in her fist, in the case of his demise, she'd inherit his books? How thoughtful. No doubt his choice of reading matter would fascinate her.

Then she caught herself. Hadn't she had similar thoughts regarding his choice of music? She'd been pleasantly surprised on that one. What if.... Bidden by curiosity, she straightened the crumpled note in her hand and finished reading. "Particularly enjoyed the new Ludlum. Why not try it?"

Indeed she'd had every intention of doing just that when she'd bought the book and put it in her own bag to bring to St. Barts. He liked adventure, did he? But then he probably lived it, while she was content to read it on occasion. With a wry headshake, she opened the bag on the table and removed, one by one, the small cartons. Langouste creole, potato puffs, fresh pastry—from La Rotisserie, no doubt. Impressed by his apparent familiarity with the offerings of the island, she wondered for an instant whether he'd been on St. Barts before. Perhaps on another job? With another woman?

Fortunately at the moment hunger was a far greater force than jealousy. Setting aside all thought of Oliver and his lively if dubious past, she ate. Then read. Then slept, awakening only once, well before midnight, to hear movement on the upper level before smiling softly and closing her eyes again.

WITH THE SUN RISING BRIGHTLY, Sunday promised to be as pleasant a day as Saturday had been. Once more Leslie spent the morning on the beach. This day, however, even before she'd been able to drag herself from the sand to get a drink and a bite for lunch, she was brought to attention by the sound of footsteps on the planks leading down from the terrace. Looking up from where she lay on her stomach, she saw Oliver approaching, a large open basket in one hand, a blanket in the other.

"Hi," he said, placing the basket on the sand and spreading out the blanket. "How're you doing?"

"Not bad," she answered cautiously. She half wondered if she should excuse herself and give him his turn on the beach, then was too intrigued watching him unpack the basket to budge. "What have you got?"

"A picnic." He cast her a fleeting eye. "Hungry?"

"A little."

"Good." Within a matter of minutes, the blanket was spread with plates bearing a thick wedge of cheese, an assortment of fresh fruit, a loaf of French bread and a carafe of white wine. When he extracted two glasses, filled them and handed one to her, she accepted it graciously.

"Thanks."

"*De nada.*"

"*Rien,*" she corrected softly.

"Excuse me?"

"*Rien.* The island's French." Reaching out, she touched the bread with one finger. "Still warm? Don't tell me you baked it yourself."

"I won't," he said jauntily, producing a knife and moving to attack the loaf. "Actually—" he made a neat cut and handed her a slice, then made a similar incision in the cheese "—it was baked in a charming little bakery."

Sitting up, she grinned. "I know." Many times had she visited that very one. "But how did you? Have you been here before?"

"To St. Barts?" He popped a grape into his mouth, started to toss her one, then, seeing that her hands were full, leaned forward to press it between her lips. "Nope. But I read...and ask. Even guidebooks can be quite informative." Stretching his legs out and crossing them at the ankles, he leaned back on his elbow and took a sip of his wine.

He was wearing bathing trunks, black ones this time with a white stripe down each hip. If anything, his bare skin had an even richer tone than it had had the day before—richer and warmer and all the more tempting to touch. Stuffing a hunk of break into her mouth, Leslie chewed forcefully. Only when she'd swallowed did she give a despairing, "Hmmph! Guidebooks. You're right. They give away every secret worth keeping. As a matter of fact, when we first started coming here, St. Barts itself was a secret. For Americans, at least. Now, Gustavia's that much more crowded. Things have changed."

"It's still quite beautiful." His gaze slipped down the nearby stretch of beach. "And very private here."

Tearing her eyes from the dashing silver wings behind his ears, she followed his gaze. "Mmmmm. We're lucky."

He offered her a slice of cheese before helping himself to one. "You don't like crowds?" he asked, taking a bite as he waited for her reply.

"I don't mind them. I mean, I guess they're unavoidable at home. If one wants the pluses of a big city, one has to be willing to put up with the minuses."

"You live right in the city?"

She shook her head. "On the island."

"Is that where you teach?"

"Um hmm."

He paused to put a piece of cheese on his bread, ate it, then washed it down with his wine. Then he sat back and turned his avid gaze on her. "How did you get started?"

"Teaching?"

"Mmmm."

"I started in the city, as a matter of fact. It seemed like a good enough place to begin. I knew I wanted to work at the preschool level and, with the growing number of women working, there were preschool centers cropping up all over the place. After a year, though, I realized that . . . well . . . I wanted to be a little farther out."

"Away from your family?"

He was right on the button. "Uh huh."

"You don't like your family?"

"I love my family," she countered quickly. "It's just that . . . I needed some distance. And there were other challenges. . . ."

"Such as . . . ?"

She faced him squarely, filled with conviction. "Such as meeting the as-yet-untapped need in the suburbs.

There had already been a slew of day-care centers established there, also to meet the need of the working woman. But those centers did just that: they met the women's needs rather than those of the kids themselves. What was required was something a step above day care, a very controlled environment in which children could learn rather than simply pass the time." She paused to sip her wine. Oliver quickly lifted the carafe and added more to her glass.

"So you found something there?"

"I made something there. Another woman and I set up a small center in a room we rented in a church, put together what we thought to be a stimulating curriculum, found a super gal to teach with us, and it worked. We incorporated a year later, opened second and third branches in neighboring towns the following year. Last fall we opened our fourth. Two more are in the planning stages."

He cocked a brow. "Not bad . . . for a teacher."

"Hmmph. Sometimes I wonder about that. There are times when the managerial end supersedes everything." Then she smiled. "But I do love it. Both teaching and managing."

"You love kids?"

"Mmmm." She tore off the corner of a piece of bread and ate it. "They're such honest little creatures. Something's on their minds and they say it. Something bothers them and they cry. No pretense at all. It's delightful."

"Doesn't say much for us big creatures, does it?"

"Nope." She reached for another grape, tipped her face up to the sun and closed her eyes as she savored the grape's sweet juice. "This is great. Thanks. I do love a picnic."

"So you said."

She blushed, recalling her stormy outburst. "So I did."

"That's pretty."

She opened her eyes to find Oliver's gaze warming her. "What is?"

"Your color."

"It's the wine. Or the sun." Far be it from her to admit that his presence might have an effect.

"You look good. You sound good. Your cold really is better."

"Yes, doctor," she mocked, then held her breath, mockery fast forgotten beneath the power of his lambent gaze. His heat reached into her, stirring her blood, quickening her pulse. She wondered whether any woman could be immune to this silent command of his, a command as vocal in his eyes as in the long, sinuous strain of his body. She bit her lip and looked away, but he was one step ahead, bounding to his feet and heading for the surf.

"I need a dip," he muttered on the run, leaving Leslie to admire his athletic grace as he hit the water and dived.

"You'll get a cramp," she murmured to the breeze alone, for he was well out of earshot, intent on stroking swiftly from shore. She glanced back at the food spread on the blanket, then up at the house. Old habits died hard, but he was trying. And he was sweet. Dinner last night, a picnic today. He really *had* left her alone most of the time. Once more it occurred to her to simply disappear and leave him in peace; he'd obviously had something quite different in mind for his vacation than the innocent cohabitation she'd agreed to. But he'd suggested it, and he could leave at any time, she reasoned, though she found the thought vaguely disturbing.

With a sigh of confusion, she settled back on her towel, closed her eyes and gave herself up to the soft caress of the sun. It was far less complicated than any man, she mused. Less complicated...less satisfying.

Even now, with her body alive in heretofore forgotten crannies, she pondered the risks of each. While the sun could cause skin cancer, a man could break her heart. Yet here she lay, complacent as a basking lizard, taking her chances on the goodness of the sun. Could she take her chances with Oliver?

What she needed, she mused, was Oliver-block— something to optimize the pleasure and minimize the risk of overexposure to such a potently virile man. Did such a thing exist? She laughed aloud. It was the wine. Straight to her head. The wine....

Moments later Oliver emerged from the sea. Eyes still closed, Leslie listened as he panted toward the blanket, caught up the towel he'd brought inside the basket, rubbed it across his chest and face, then settled down on the sand by her side. For a brief instant she felt her skin tingle and knew he was looking at her.

"All right?" he asked softly.

"All right," she answered, then relaxed when he closed his eyes.

They lay together in a companionable silence, rising every so often to munch on the goodies he'd brought, to dip in the water and cool off, to turn in the sun or move into the shade and read. It was Leslie who excused herself first, gathering her things and returning to the house, phoning to have a rental car delivered, then showering. Donning a strappy yellow sundress and sandals, she drove into town to eat at a small port-side café.

The sunset was beautiful, tripping over the harbor with its pert gathering of assorted small boats. Time and again, though, her eye was drawn to the couples surrounding her at other tables on the open-air terrace. Healthy and tanned, they sat close together, hands entwined, heads bent toward one another with an air of intimacy she envied. She wondered where they'd come from, whether they were married, whether the happiness they appeared to have captured was simply a product of the romantic setting or whether the setting had enhanced something that had been good from the start.

Leaving without dessert, she returned to the villa, only to find it empty. For a time she wandered from room to room making a pretense of admiring the fresh tropical decor before she settled at last in the den with the book she'd abandoned earlier. This was what she'd wanted, she reminded herself pointedly. Peace and solitude.

Three times she read the same page before finally absorbing its words.

BY MONDAY MORNING her cold was nothing more than a memory. She rose in time to spot the dark-haired figure swimming in the early-morning sun, and, not daring to join him, retreated to the kitchen to fix a breakfast of bacon and eggs and muffins. There was more than enough for two. Quickly eating her share, she left the rest on the stove and returned to her room. Then, on a whim, she packed up a towel, a wide-brimmed straw hat, her lotion and a book and went into town to buy a newspaper, which she read over a cup of coffee before heading for the public beach.

Spreading her towel on the sand, she shimmied out of her terry cover-up, then, with a glance around to assure herself that the mode hadn't changed, gracefully removed her bikini top and lay down in the sun.

It felt wonderful, as she'd known it would. Strange that she could do this so easily on a public beach, while she'd persisted in wearing her one-piece suit in the privacy of the villa. But the villa wasn't totally private this time round, was it?

Squinting in the sun, she wrestled her lotion from the bag and squirted a generous dollop onto her stomach. It spread easily beneath her hands. She worked it up past her ribs, around and over her breasts to her shoulders, finally smoothing the remainder down her arms before lying back. Better. Warm. Relaxing.

Why *couldn't* she do this at the villa? Was there truly safety in numbers? Peeking through the shadow of her lashes, she scanned the growing crowd. The bodies were beautiful, few of them covered by more than slim bands of material at their hips. Men and women. Lean and fit. Well, she was lean and fit, too. What objection could she have to Oliver's seeing her like this?

Oliver was lean and fit. She recalled how he'd looked this morning with the sun glancing off his limbs as he swam. She recalled how he'd looked yesterday, lying beside her on the sand. His shoulders were sturdy and tanned, his hips narrow, his legs well formed. She liked the soft matting of hair that roughened those legs, the broader patch on his chest, the tapering line down his stomach. His body was every bit as beautiful as that of any man on the beach today. And his hands—those hands that had so deftly poured wine, sliced cheese, popped a single grape into her mouth—had those fingers touched her lips? She remembered how easily they'd circled her wrist to tug her back down to the sand. What might they have been like spreading lotion on her body . . . ?

To her dismay, she felt her breasts grow taut. Peering down in embarrassment, she flipped angrily over onto her stomach and silently tore into herself for the foolishness of her thoughts. Was she that starved for the touch of a man? True, it had been a long time since she'd been reckless enough to trust one to the point of making love. But she'd never known the kind of frustration that would make her body respond out of sheer imagination. Opening one eye, she skimmed the bodies nearby, pausing at that of one attractive man, then another. Nothing. *Damn him!*

Defiantly she rolled over once more and concentrated on her life back home. The preschool centers were thriving. Six by next fall...quite an accomplishment. What now? Should she continue to teach? Go back to school for a business degree? Focus on the managerial skills she'd inadvertently picked up? There were many options, not the least of which was to take Tony up on his offer of signing on with the corporation. Even in spite of the distance she purposely placed between it and herself, she was neither deaf nor blind. Had she not caught talk at family gatherings of the corporation's spreading interests, she had certainly read of them in the newspapers. There were new divisions forming all the time, any one of which she could take over if she showed the slightest inclination.

But she didn't. And she wouldn't. There was something about high power and the almighty buck that stuck in her craw. Misplaced values. Misguided loyalties. Marriages of convenience rather than love.

Look at Tony. He'd married Laura because she'd promised to be the kind of wife every chief executive needed. Only problem was that every *other* chief executive needed her, or wanted her...or simply took her, so it seemed.

Sensing the dry, parched feel to her legs, Leslie sat up and smoothed lotion on them liberally, then lay down again. And Brenda—she was working on number two. Number one had been her high-school sweetheart and had unfortunately developed a penchant for gambling away every cent she earned. Poor Brenda. John had been a disappointment. Perhaps Larry would be better for her.

And then there was Diane. Slim, petite Diane, who'd wanted nothing more than to be a gymnastics star until she'd discovered that all the money in the world couldn't buy her the gold. Unable to settle for silver or

bronze, she'd quit gymnastics and, by way of consolation, had been awarded the sporting-goods division of
the corporation.

From the start she'd been in over her head. Even Tony
had seen that. When she'd quite opportunely fallen in
love with Brad Weitz, himself a senior vice-president of
his family's development firm, things looked good.
What with Brad's business acumen and that of the circle
of lesser executives he helped Diane gather, she was able
to focus her own attentions on the content of the Parish
line, rather than its high-level management.

Unfortunately, while the business flourished, her
marriage floundered. Brad wandered, always returning
to soothe Diane's injured pride, yet inevitably straying
again before long. More than once Diane had eyed Leslie in envy at the latter's unencumbered state.

If only she knew, Leslie reflected wryly as she turned
onto her stomach and tuned in to the sounds of the gentle Caribbean air. They were soft sounds—the murmur
of easy conversation from parties nearby, the light
laughter of those near the water's edge, the occasional
cry of a bird flying overhead. How delightful it was to
be here, she mused, to leave that other world where it
was. Soon enough she'd be back to face it again. Soon
enough she'd have to decide where she wanted to go
with her life. But for now she wanted to relax and enjoy.
That was all...that was all...that was all....

Lulled by the sun, she lay in a semisomnolent state,
breathing slowly and evenly, savoring anonymity and
the total absence of responsibility. When she felt hot,
she stood and unselfconsciously walked into the water,
swam about in the pale aqua surf, then returned to her
towel. Stretching out on her back, she closed her eyes. It
was divine. Thoroughly divine. She felt herself a part of
the crowd, at ease and more in the spirit of the island
than she had since she'd arrived.

Bathers came and went as the sun crept to its apex. Lathering her body frequently, Leslie knew she was beginning to blend in with the bronzed bodies all around. With a sigh, she closed her eyes and returned to her worship. Once, maybe twice a year she could do this. Any more and not only would she get bored, but her body would wrinkle like a prune. Once...maybe twice a year...it was nice....

With a self-indulgent smile on her face, she turned her head slightly to one side and peered at the world through the shade of thick, tawny lashes. Then her smile froze in place and her complacency vanished. A man lay close by, sprawled stomach down on a towel, with his head turned away. Dark brown hair with a distinct C of gray behind his ear.... *Him!* When had he come? How could he have found her? His back glistened with suntan lotion; his breathing was even. It appeared he'd been there for some time, while she'd lain half nude, oblivious to all but the sun....

For the second time that day she twisted onto her stomach in embarrassment. The first time she'd simply imagined him and her body had reacted. Now he was here, beside her. What was she going to do? Head turned away, eyes open wide, heart pounding, she examined her alternatives. She could nonchalantly slip on her top and as nonchalantly lie back down. But he'd know, and she'd feel more the coward for it. She could simply dress and leave, but then she'd be deprived of her time on the beach. She could lie where she was until he tired of the beach and left. But he wouldn't do that without a word to her, would he? Not after having so conveniently selected her body from all those others on the beach beside which to stretch his sexy six-foot-plus frame! Besides, was she supposed to lie on her stomach for the rest of the day?

There was one other alternative and, damn it, she was

going to take it. She'd come to the beach on her own and had been perfectly happy and comfortable. Oliver or no Oliver, she was going to stay. In the sun. And on her back, if she so pleased.

On a rebellious impulse, she flipped back as she'd been when first she'd spotted Oliver beside her. When her head fell his way, she gasped in genuine surprise. He was looking straight at her.

"Oliver!" she whispered, her breath in scarce supply. "You startled me!" It was the truth. Somehow she'd been counting on time to adjust to the fact of his presence.

As though relieved that she'd only been startled, he smiled gently. "I'm sorry. I didn't mean to do that." His eyes held hers without straying.

"How long have you been here?"

"Not long. Maybe fifteen, twenty minutes."

"Oh."

"Nice beach."

"Mmmm."

"Tired of yours?"

She turned down the corners of her mouth and shook her head, felt her breasts shimmy and lost her courage. As gracefully as she could—and as casually—she rolled to her stomach again. Though the move brought her all the closer to Oliver, she felt somehow let off the hook. "It's nice here once in a while," she murmured, then managed to feign a relaxed sigh. Facing him, she closed her eyes. His next words brought them open in a hurry.

"I didn't think you'd do this, Les."

She knew precisely what he meant. "Why not?"

"You seem more . . . inhibited."

"I usually am," she confessed in the same half whisper in which the rest of the conversation was being carried on. There was something intimate about their talk; Leslie found she liked the feeling.

Arching his back, he folded his arms beneath his chin. "What makes things different here?"

Had there been the faintest hint of mockery in his tone, she might have been put on the defensive instantly. But his voice remained gentle and curious, his eyes simply warm and pleased.

"I don't know. Maybe the other people. They're strangers."

"And safe?"

"I guess."

"Impersonal."

"Um hmm."

"Like...a gynecologist?"

"Come on, Oliver. What is this?"

"Just trying to understand why you'd bare yourself for them...but not for me."

"Oliver!" He had almost sounded hurt. When she opened her eyes in alarm, she indeed read that same gut-wrenching vulnerability written across his chiseled face. In response, she took her lip between her teeth. As quickly, he reached out a hand.

"Don't do that," he murmured, rubbing the tip of his forefinger against her lip until she'd released it herself. His finger lingered a moment longer in caress of her softly parted mouth. Then he put his hand on her back. The subtle incursion brought him inches closer. "God, your skin is hot. You'll be burned to a crisp."

"I'm okay." She felt strangely restful and raised no objection when he began to move his hand in a gentle kneading caress. For several seconds they just lay and stared at each other. "Oliver?"

"Mmm?"

"What's it like to model?"

His hand paused for only an instant before resuming its soothing motion. "It's...fun."

"You said that once before. But...I've always heard

talk of the trying pace—you know, hours doing the same thing over and over again. Is it like that?"

"I don't know," he said simply. "I've never had to do the same thing over and over again."

"You're that good?" She smiled in accompaniment to her teasing tone and was rewarded by his total absence of arrogance.

"No. It just . . . works."

Her thoughts joined his on the set of the Homme Premier ad. "Is it ever . . . awkward?"

"What do you mean?"

"When you . . . I mean . . . you are nude, aren't you?"

He dared a tiny grin. "Yes."

"Does it bother you?"

"I like nudity."

"So, if this were a nude beach, you would . . . ?" Her brief glance toward his trunks said it all.

"No," he murmured without hesitation.

"Why not?"

"Because it would be embarrassing."

"Embarrassing? But you've got a beautiful body!"

Again that tiny grin. "How do you know? You haven't seen it all."

Again her downward glance. "There's not much left covered."

He arched a brow. "Some men might take offense at that."

"Come on," she chided. "You knew what I meant. Would you really be embarrassed to *un*cover it?"

"On this beach . . . beside you . . . yes."

"Because of *me*?" So she wasn't the only neurotic one?

"Yes." He inched closer. His lips were a breath from hers. "I don't think I could lie quite as impassively as—" he cocked his head "—most of these other men seem to be doing. It was bad enough when I first got here and saw your car in the lot. I've been to this beach before; I knew what the style was." His hand slowed its motion, coming to a rest just beneath her armpit. Leslie felt her breasts tingle at the nearness, but she couldn't move. His eyes held hers with binding warmth. "There are lots of pretty women here, Les, but I was totally unaffected...until I saw you."

"Sounds like the lyric to a song," she teased by way of self-defense, lifting her eyes and singing, "'Til I saw you....'" Then, recalling how boldly she'd been lying on her back with her breasts bare, exposed to the sun, she blushed.

"I'm serious," he said, brushing the back of his fingers against the swell of her breast. Suddenly she was, too.

"I know," she whispered. Had his earnestness been faked, something would have given it away—the glimmer of an eye, the twitch of a mouth, the rush to offer other lofty words. Oliver's expression, however, was solemn, every feature in harmony with the intensity of his gaze. He said nothing more, simply looked at Leslie as though imprisoned by the very charm that gave credence to his claim. Only his hand moved, sliding very gently along the side of her breast, up and back, doing ragged things to her pulse, damaging things to her composure. She felt his touch through every inch of her being. Her gaze dropped to his lips.

"You're very soft," he mouthed. He slid his thumb forward until it skimmed her aureole.

Leslie caught her breath, then, swept up in the sensual magic of the moment, released it and whispered his name. It was as though her entire life had been in a state of limbo...and only now took direction once more.

HER LIPS WERE PARTED. Stealing forward, he accepted their invitation, grazing her in soft, slow mouthfuls until she closed her eyes and yielded to his quiet fire. Her insides burned, and still he teased, growing evasive between lingering kisses, forcing her mouth to be more aggressive in its search for satisfaction.

"Oliver!" she whispered, angling her body just high enough to slip his hand beneath and press it to her breast. "I can't stand this!" she gasped, watching the slow opening of his eyes.

"*You* can't stand it?" he growled hoarsely. "They're apt to arrest us in a minute." He wiggled a finger against her throbbing nipple and took pleasure in the moan she suppressed. Her fingers tightened over his, yet she didn't pull his hand away. She couldn't. His touch felt far too good, as though that of a long-lost lover who'd just come home. Feeling suddenly light-headed, she gave a mischievous grin.

"Do you think they would?" She cast a surreptitious glance around. "I mean, there have to be other people fooling around here." Then she frowned. "Why don't I ever see it?"

"Because you're not a voyeur," he returned simply. "If you were looking, you'd find it."

"You did?" she asked, eyes alight, curious. "Come on, Oliver," she whispered conspiratorially. She tugged his hand upward and cushioned it against her cheek so that his arm fully crossed her nakedness. Their bodies were snug, side by side. She felt wonderfully alive. "Tell me."

"I will not. It might give you ideas."

"Ideas? What ideas?"

When he grinned, the groove at the corner of his mouth deepened. She hadn't noticed it before; it had a lazy sensuality to it. "Now if I told you that, you'd know what I've seen. I think I'd better go back to sleep." Turning his head away, he raised his hips and resettled them in a bid to ease his discomfort. Leslie appreciated the gesture, appreciated even more his attempt at self-control, appreciated most of all that strong, hairy arm that tickled her where it counted.

"Sleep?" she challenged. "Is that what you were doing?"

He turned back until their heads were intimately close. "No. I suppose not. I was lying here thinking. . . ." His tone was up; he seemed ready to go on. Then, expelling a soft breath, he simply repeated the word with a proper period at its end. "Thinking."

"Are you pleased with St. Barts?" she asked, nestling more comfortably against the arm he seemed in no hurry to remove.

"Yes." An affirmation it was, yet it dangled in the air.

"You don't sound convinced."

"Oh, it's fine."

"But?"

"Just about everyone's coupled up. It makes me feel lonely."

She sent him a look of doubt. "Does it mean that much to you to be with a date?"

"For the sake of a date? No way. For the sake of pleasant talk and easy companionship, yes. That's what I see here—on the beach, in shops and cafés. Warmth. I envy it."

"I know the feeling," she murmured half to herself as she recalled similar feelings she'd harbored the night before. She lifted her head for an instant to look forward. "Who do you think they are, Oliver? Friends? Lovers? Husbands and wives?"

His gaze followed hers, lighting on a couple lying on the sand several yards away. "Some of each, I suppose." He tossed his chin at the pair. "They're married."

"Oh?"

"Sure. See his wedding band?"

"Where's hers?"

"Oh. Hmm, that shoots that theory."

"Oliver?"

He settled his head down again, returning his mouth to within a whisper of hers. "Um hmm?"

"Were you ever married?"

"No."

"Why not?"

"Never wanted to."

"Not even for the sake of that warmth?"

"The woman, not the marriage, brings the warmth."

"True. But what about kids?" Strange. By stereotype, she'd assume he'd have no interest in children. Somehow, though, she could easily picture him with a brood. "Wouldn't you marry for the sake of having them?"

"A bad marriage for the sake of kids can be disastrous."

"You could have a good marriage."

"I could...I suppose. It's been hard finding good women—" he smirked "—what with my job and all."

She nodded. "Your job and all."

"How about you?"

"*My* job's no problem."

"Then why aren't you married? You seem like a warm, affectionate sort." He moved one finger ever so slightly against her cheek. "And you love kids. Wouldn't you like your own?"

"To quote you, 'A bad marriage for the sake of kids can be disastrous.'"

"To quote you back, 'You could have a good marriage.'"

She grew more serious. "If only. It seems that wherever I look I see divorces piling up. Divorces, or couples in the throes of counseling or those who are simply miserable. Maybe you don't see it, or maybe you take it for granted in your line of work, but I see it every day and it bothers me. Not only has my family struck out, but many of the kids at the centers are products of broken homes. And many of them are suffering terribly."

Oliver studied the look of anguish on her face. "But now you're getting onto the issue of kids again. What about the marriages to start with? Why is it that they're not working?"

She thought for a minute, then shrugged. "I don't know. Too much ambition. Too little honesty. Too much independence. Too little trust. Maybe it's the times, and what we're going through is an emotional evolution of sorts. Maybe love has to take on different meanings to make it feasible in this day and age. Take that couple over there. For all we know, his wife may be off with someone, too. But if she's in love and they're in love, and all four are happy, far be it from us to criticize them, particularly if we've got nothing better."

As Oliver pondered her words, his brow furrowed. "You condone infidelity?"

"No, not really." She was frowning, too. "Maybe what I'm saying is that love is the most important factor, that it makes allowance for other slips. Only problem is that where love is involved, those other slips can cause terrible, terrible pain. . . ."

"You sound very sure."

"I am."

"You've had personal experience with that kind of pain?"

Realizing she'd strayed far from the beaten path and in a direction she loathed, she shrugged. "It's not important." She sighed and forced a lighter smile. "Besides, it all may be an illusion anyway. These people may not be in love, they might simply be swept up in the atmosphere of this place. There's something about a tropical island in the middle of winter...."

"Something daring, like lying on a beach half nude?"

In that instant, the more serious discussion was shelved. Leslie grinned. "Something like that."

"Why don't you turn over?" he teased.

She fought fire with fire, enjoying the banter. "Why don't *you*?"

"Because I keep thinking of *your* doing it and I get... hot and bothered."

"Hot and bothered. Interesting."

"Tell you what. I'll go down the beach a way and pretend you're not here. If you do the same, we'll be all right."

"I don't know." She wavered, reluctant to lose his company. "Maybe we could do it here...."

His eyes gaped. "Do what?"

"Lie cool and comfortable...." She felt so very close to him that it seemed absurd, this modesty of hers. Avoiding his gaze, she released his arm and turned over with slow and studied nonchalance. "There," she sighed, eyes closed, body aware of far more than the sun. "Your turn."

He offered a pithy oath beneath his breath, then coughed away the frog in his throat. "I think I'll take that walk."

"Don't go," she whispered, turning her head and opening her eyes. "I mean, it's really all right. There's no reason you can't stay here. It's all a matter...of the mind."

His eyes pierced hers, then seared a path to her breasts. "Is that all it is?" he asked, his voice thick. "A matter of the mind?"

Leslie felt his gaze as long, sinewed fingers caressing her fullness, belying her claim. Her breathing was already disturbed when he pushed himself up on his forearms and put his mouth to her ear.

"You've got beautiful breasts, Leslie."

"So do three-quarters of the women on this beach."

"I'm not looking at their breasts. I'm looking at yours."

She felt the truth of his words. Her breasts were ready to explode. "Well, you shouldn't be."

He ignored her. "Need some lotion? I'm great at spreading lotion up over—"

"Oliver!" she exclaimed in strangled protest. "You could try, at least—"

"I'm trying. I'm trying."

"Sure. To get me aroused." She gave him a withering stare. "Now try to get me *un*aroused."

"What fun would that be?"

"Oliver," she warned, growing frustrated in, oh, so many ways, "you promised you'd leave me alone. You promised you wouldn't push."

Before her beseeching expression, he grew serious. "I did, didn't I?" She nodded, her face inches below his. "Then," he began slowly, a look of regret in his mocha gaze, "I guess I'd better take that walk after all." He kissed the tip of her nose and was on his feet before Leslie could respond. But it was just as well. Bracing herself on her elbows, she watched him jog toward the water, submerge completely in the waves, swim off his own arousal, then emerge and walk thoughtfully down the beach.

She would have loved to have gone with him. It would have been nice, walking side by side with the lace of the surf curling at their feet. It would have been nice to have talked more. She enjoyed talking with him. He was easygoing, quick to smile and curious. She would have assumed the beautiful model-type to be self-centered, yet he wasn't. He seemed far more interested in hearing her thoughts than in impressing her with his own. Come to think of it, he'd spoken little of himself in the discussions they'd had.

With a sigh, she dropped back to the towel. In this, too, it was probably just as well. Given the source of his income, the less she knew about his life-style the better. Hmmph, she mused, he had all the lines. Beautiful breasts. . .attracted to no body but hers—baloney! He was a pro, and hanky-panky or no, he was still on the job. The only problem was that she wanted to believe him. She wanted to believe that he found her breasts beautiful, that he was more attracted to her than to any other woman on the beach. She wanted to believe. . . how she wanted to believe. . . .

Abruptly sitting up, she put on her bikini top, tugged on her terry cover-up and gathered her things together. She'd had enough of the beach for now. A long, slow drive around the island would clear her brain. That was what she needed—a long, slow drive.

It filled the bill. By the time she returned to the villa she had her mind in working order once more. She was Leslie Parish, loner, spending the week at her family's villa. Oliver Ames just happened, by a quirk of fate attributable to her brother Tony and worthy of no further mention, to be staying at the villa as well. That was all. Each went his own way, did his own thing. Period. She had it all straightened out. . .which made it doubly hard for her to understand her continuing restlessness.

After her return, she fell asleep on her bed. At some point during that time, Oliver quietly returned to the villa. When she awoke, she found his sprawled form spilling over one of the terrace chairs. He was reading a book.

Wearing the one-piece terry sunsuit she'd put on after her shower, she walked slowly out onto the terrace, gave Oliver's shoulder a gentle squeeze of hello as she passed, then stood with her back to him at the railing overlooking the beach. When several minutes passed and still she didn't speak, Oliver took the first step.

"You got back okay. I was worried."

She turned to lean against the wooden rail. "You shouldn't have been." But it touched her nonetheless. "I took a drive." He nodded, and she felt a tinge of remorse that she'd left the beach without a word. His thoughts were back there, too.

He dared a faint smile. "I had trouble finding my towel . . . without your breasts to mark the spot."

"Oliver . . ." she pleaded.

"Sorry." He nodded once, then schooled his expression to the proper degree of sobriety. "Couldn't resist that."

"I'm sure."

"I did miss you, though," he said, suddenly and fully sincere. "It was fun lying like that . . . talking. . . ."

Hadn't she had similar thoughts? She looked down at her bare feet and crossed her ankles. "Uh, that was what I wanted to talk to you about."

Far more jumpy than she might have imagined, Oliver grew instantly alert. He held up a hand and shook his head. "Listen, Leslie, it was no big thing. I wasn't out chasing you or anything. I mean, I'd been to that beach the day before, and when I saw your car I thought I'd look for you. I didn't mean to pester. Hell, I was only teasing about your breasts. . . ." His voice trailed off when he caught her amused expression. "What's so funny?"

"You are. When you get defensive, you're adorable.

But that's beside the point. I was just wondering if—well, there's this quiet restaurant in Gustavia...very classy...and I thought, well, I don't really feel like going alone what with everyone else coupled up, as you said." She paused for a breath, wondering why he didn't come to her aid rather than sitting there with a bewildered look on his face. "What I was wondering," she began again, "was whether you'd like to have dinner with me."

"Yes," he answered instantly.

"I mean, you can think about it. I...I can't offer anything afterward. Just dinner."

A broad smile illuminated his face. "That's fine. Dinner will be just fine."

She took a deep breath and smiled. "Good. I'll make reservations for eighty-thirty?"

"Great."

She nodded, feeling awkward again. Pushing off from the railing, she headed for the beach. "See ya then."

THE EVENING TURNED OUT to be worth every bit of her hemming and hawing in issuance of the invitation. She'd wanted stimulating company; stimulating company was what she got. Looking particularly handsome in a navy blue side-buttoned shirt and white slacks, Oliver proved to be an absolutely charming dinner partner. Ever solicitous to her whim, he deftly steered the conversation from one topic to the next. Not only was he conversant in the fine points of Wall Street, he was easily able to match Leslie's knowledge of politics, as well. He got her to talk more about her work, showing genuine interest and a flair for understanding the tenuous link between parent, child and teacher. Only when once or twice on impulse Leslie shot a personal question at him did he pull back. She assumed it was standard practice—the refusal to allow a client past a certain point. And though she was curious as to what made him tick, she appreciated the reminder about the nature of their relationship. With such an attentive and attractive man sitting elbow to elbow with her in the intimate confines of the small French restaurant, it was far, far too easy to forget . . . .

TUESDAY WAS A DAY FOR REMEMBERING, a quiet day, a restful day. Leslie saw Oliver only in passing, and then but once, at noontime. They exchanged quiet smiles and hellos. He explained that he wanted to pick up something for his sister back home and asked for her advice. Stifling the urge to ask all about his sister, she suggested a small boutique in Gustavia, from among whose selection of hand-blocked prints and clothing she was sure he'd find something. Then he was off, with nary a word about the evening before.

Just as well, she told herself again. Just as well. She'd come here to be alone. Alone was what she'd get.

Unfortunately, alone became lonely at some point around dinnertime. With no sign of Oliver, she grilled a piece of fresh fish, sliced and marinated vegetables, made herself an exotic-looking drink, which was little more than rum and coke dressed up in a coconut shell with an orange slice across the top, and ate by herself on the beach. It was there that, long after the sun had set, Oliver found her.

"Leslie?" he called from the terrace. "Leslie?"

"Here, Oliver!" she answered, her heart suddenly beating more lightly. "On the beach!"

A random cloud had wandered in front of the moon. It took him a minute to find his way down. Only when he stood before her on the sand did the silvery light reemerge. "You're eating here . . . in the dark?" he asked, spying the tray behind her.

She looked up from where she sat, knees bent, arms

crossed around them. She wore a gauzy blouse and skirt, the latter ruffling around her calves. "It wasn't dark when I ate. I've just been sitting here thinking." For a minute she feared he would simply nod and, finding her safe, return to the house. To her relief, he hunkered down beside her.

"Mind the company?" he asked, suddenly cautious.

"No," she breathed softly. "As a matter of fact, it's kind of lonely here. The company would be nice."

"You should have called. I'd have come."

"You weren't here."

"I've been back for at least an hour and a half."

"Where all did you go?" He wore shorts and a shirt and looked devastatingly handsome.

"Oh—" he gazed out at the sea "—I was in Gustavia, then rode around for a while."

"Find something for your sister?"

"Uh huh."

"Have you eaten?"

"I grabbed something in town."

She nodded, feeling superfluous, then took a fast breath. "Hey, if you've got something to do. I don't want to keep you. . . ."

"You're not. I was the one who offered, remember?" His voice lowered. "You look pretty. Very . . . feminine."

Her blush was hidden by the night. She shrugged. "It's nice to wear something like this every so often." Last night, her dress had been as soft, but more sleek— to lend her an air of confidence and sophistication. Tonight she looked and felt vulnerable.

Attuned to her mood, Oliver kept his voice on a gentle keel. "It must be appreciated. I'm envious of those men you date at home."

Her heart skipped a beat. "You don't need to be. There aren't an awful lot of them."

"But you do date...."

"Only when necessary."

He frowned. "What do you mean?"

"Just that," she returned frankly. "There are certain...
social obligations to be fulfilled. Birthday parties, open-
ings, receptions—that type thing. It's sometimes easier
being with someone than without."

For a moment, only the gentle lapping of the waves
broke the silence of the night. When Oliver spoke again,
his voice held a deadly calm. "Was that what you felt
last night?"

"Oh, no!" she exclaimed without pretense. "Last night
was something different! Last night...it was...I
wanted it...." She stared wide-eyed at Oliver until at
last he reached over and took her hand in his. Only then
did she relax.

"I'm glad, Les. I enjoyed myself last night. More than
I have in a very long time."

"A very long time?" she teased. "Doesn't say much
for all those other women."

His fingers tightened around hers instants before his
taut voice rang out. "There haven't been all those other
women, Leslie. I think it's about time we clear that up.
I'm not a gigolo."

"I never said you were," she countered weakly.

"But you've thought it. And don't deny it, because
my thumb's on your pulse, keeping track of your lies."

"That's fear you feel. You're frightening me." Instantly his grip eased, though her hand was as much a prisoner as ever.

"Have you ever thought I was a gigolo?"

"I, uh...."

"Yes or no."

"Yes. Well, what was I to think? You were my birthday present. My brother *bought* you for the week. For
me. Isn't it pretty much the same thing?"

To her relief, Oliver's voice had gentled again. "I suppose. If it were true. But it's not."

"What's not?" She felt a glimmer of hope. "Tony didn't hire you?"

"Tony called me, explained the situation and proposed I come. Aside from free use of this house, everything has come from my own pocket."

Leslie's mind had begun to whirl, her relief nearly as overwhelming as her embarrassment. Not knowing what to say, she blithely lashed out at Tony. "That cheapskate! I mean, I know that you probably do very well modeling, but I'd have thought that if the plan was his the least he could do was foot the bill!" Taking Oliver off guard, she tore her hand from his and tucked it tightly into her lap. She was sitting cross-legged now, the folds of her skirt gathered loosely between her legs. "I'm not sure whether to be more angry for his having gypped you or undersold me!"

"You weren't sold, Leslie! That's what I'm trying to tell you! I needed a vacation. Tony simply suggested a spot. As for the practical joke, well, that was to be frosting on the cake."

"Frosting, indeed," she mumbled. "All along I've assumed this was nothing more than a business proposition for you. But you speak very comfortably of Tony—do you know my brother?"

Taking a deep breath, Oliver settled on the sand facing her. "I met him about a year ago. We play tennis every now and again."

"Was it Tony who set up the Homme Premier thing?"

"No. As a matter of fact, it was sheer coincidence that the ad ran in his magazine."

"I see." Lowering her chin, she scowled at her skirt. She did see—more now, at least, than she had before. Yet while one part of her was elated to learn that Oliver

Ames wasn't the horrible playboy for hire she'd thought him to be, the other part was mortified.

"Les...?" came the soft voice opposite her. "What is it?"

"I feel foolish," she whispered. "Really foolish."

"But why?"

She looked up then, her eyes round and luminous. "I thought you were a gigolo." She paused, offering a spitting aside, "God, that word's disgusting!" before resuming her self-castigation. "You must think I'm a perfect ass...what with some of the things I said."

"Actually," he grinned, "they were amusing."

"At my expense!"

"At mine. I was a good sport, don't you think?"

"I think you could have told me the truth. Good sport, hah!" Swiveling on the sand, she turned away from him.

"Hey," he crooned, reaching out to take her arm. "Come on. There was no harm done. Besides, you really didn't say very much that didn't apply to a model as well. I've never thought less of you...for any of it."

She wanted to believe him, but simply shook her head. "I felt so humiliated when I first arrived, thinking that Tony was really paying you to keep me company."

"Sweetheart, nobody pays for my time in chunks like that," he drawled, then cleared his throat when Leslie eyed him questioningly. "I'm a free agent. I don't like to spend more than one day at a stretch on any given job. This is no job. Believe me, if I hadn't wanted to come here, I wouldn't have. Likewise—" his hand caressed her arm "—I could have left at any time."

Trying to assimilate this altered image of Oliver, she felt confused and unsure. A model. Just a model. Was that so awful? It was still a world away, and in many ways the epitome of all she'd fought for years. Illusion. Grand pretense. Wasn't that what advertising was all about? But then there was this man—his face, his smile, the vulnerability about him that mirrored her own....

Turning her head, she looked up at him. Then, without thinking, she rolled to her knees, put her arms around his neck and held him tightly. Only after several seconds did she feel his arms complete the circle.

"What's this for?" he whispered hoarsely.

She closed her eyes and hung on a minute longer, drinking in every bit of his closeness before finally loosening her grip and sinking back against his hands. "An apology...and thanks."

"Thanks?"

"For not accepting money to pleasure me."

His voice deepened. "Am I...pleasuring you?"

She could barely breathe, the pull of him was so strong. "Yes. I've enjoyed having you here."

"Now, that's a concession," he said softly, then shifted to lower her to the sand. With one hand he propped himself over her, with the other very gently tucked her hair behind her ear. "You are beautiful, Leslie," he murmured. "Even if there had been all of those other women you'd imagined, I'd still have thought you to be the best."

"Must be the full moon addling your mind."

"You don't think you're beautiful?"

"No. Oh, I make a nice appearance. But beautiful?" She shook her head against his hand, liking the feel of its tethered strength. "No."

"Well, you are. And if you didn't turn all those guys away so quick, they'd be the ones telling you, not me."

"They tell me, they tell me! It's so boring when you know it's all part of the game."

Oliver's body grew tense, his eyes darker. "This isn't, Les. I mean it. To me, you are beautiful. Do you believe me?"

Strangely, she did. "I must be as crazy as you."

"Not crazy. Simply...." He never finished what he was going to say, but instead lowered his head and took her lips in a kiss that was crazy and heady and bright. "Ahh, Leslie," he gasped, pausing for air before returning to take what was so warmly, so freely, so avidly offered.

Reeling beneath the heat of his kiss, Leslie could do nothing but respond in kind. Her lips parted, giving the sweet moisture of her mouth, the wet stroking of her tongue into Oliver's thirsty possession. With the freedom she'd craved—forever, it seemed—she thrust her fingers into the thick hair behind his ears and savored its vibrant lushness as she held him all the closer.

"Mmmmmmm, Oliver," she whispered on a ragged breath when he left her lips and began to press slow kisses against the fragrant pulse of her neck.

"You smell so sweet—" he breathed deeply against her skin "—so sweet."

Then he raised his head and kissed her again, moving his lips with adoration, his hands with utter care, his body with the gentleness she'd come to expect of him. He was lean and strong, his long frame branding its readied state on her, telling her of his need, inflaming her own. If this was illusion, she mused, it was divine illusion indeed.

"I need you, Les," he moaned, leaving one of his hard thighs thrust between hers as he slid to his side to free a hand for exploration. "I need to touch you here—" his hands grew bolder, spreading over her waist and ribs "—and here." Claiming her breasts with tender strength, his fingers circled her fullness, sending corresponding spirals of fire through her. "Feel good?"

She closed her eyes and nodded. "Oh, yes—" When his palm passed over her nipple, taunting it into a tight nub, she moaned and strained upward. Then, eyes flying open, she pressed her hand on top of his to stop its motion. "My God, Oliver, there's no end...."

"There *is* an end, sweet. I'll show you."

He held her gaze; she held her breath. Slowly he released first one, then another of the buttons of her blouse and slipped his large hand inside. "I wanted to do this yesterday on the beach," he whispered, fingering her flesh, sensitizing her to his touch.

"I know. . . ." She sucked in a loud breath.

"Nice?" His fingers worked a heated magic, making everything feel so very right.

"Mmmmmm. . . Oliver?"

He put his lips to the upper swell of her breast. "What, sweet?"

"My breasts. . ." she managed through a daze of passion, yielding to a nagging force. "You said you were only teasing. . . that they were more appealing than the others on the beach. Were you?"

He drew his head up to eye her in earnest. "No, I wasn't teasing. I meant what I said, Leslie. Your body affects me in a way no other can." Leaning forward, he nudged her blouse farther aside, then took her nipple into his mouth and kissed it reverently.

She shuddered, sighed, arched ever so slightly closer. "I'm glad. I don't like to be teased. . . not about a thing like that." Her voice grew stronger. "Not about a thing like. . . us."

A nearly imperceptible quiver worked its disquieting way through Oliver's long, taut limbs. He stilled for an instant, then slowly, reluctantly disengaged his mouth from her breast and gave a final kiss to the hollow of her throat before setting his fingers to the task of restoring order to her blouse. "We have to talk," he murmured against the warm skin of her cheek. "We have to talk."

Very slowly, Leslie realized that the source of her pleasure was gone. With uncertainty coming fast on the heels of passion, her limbs felt like rubber. When Oliver lifted her to a sitting position, she docilely sat. Her eyes were wide, her voice breathy. "What is it?" she asked, fearing she'd done something dreadfully wrong.

"We have to talk."

"You've said that . . . three times."

"I also said I'd leave you alone. I haven't done that."

Hearing the self-reproach in his voice, Leslie was fast to shoulder the blame. "What happened just now was more my fault than yours. I was the one who threw herself into your arms."

"That's beside the point," he grumbled, then shoved a hand through his hair and took several steadying breaths. "Listen, maybe you're right. Maybe it is the full moon." Standing, he reached to pull her up. "Come on. Let's go inside. I could use a drink." One-handedly scooping up the tray that held the remnants of her dinner, he motioned for Leslie to precede him.

She did. It took everything she was worth, but she did, and with each step she came closer to the understanding of what had nearly happened. Even now her breath came in shallow bursts, her legs shook, the knot deep within clamored for more. But her mind, ahh, her mind delivered a batch of far different messages.

Passing through the kitchen, she made straight for the living room, seeking shelter in a deeply cushioned rattan armchair to weather the storm. For there was bound to be a storm of some kind, she knew. It had been building from the moment she'd arrived last Friday, had been denied outlet moments before, now ached for release.

Through troubled eyes she watched Oliver approach the bar. As attractive as he looked in his jersey and slacks, their fine fit fairly broadcast his tension. His shoulders were rigid, his back ramrod straight, his legs taut. He poured himself a brandy, shot a glance over his shoulder, poured a second drink, then crossed the room and handed her one. While he tipped his snifter and took a drink, she merely watched the swirl of the amber liquid in her own glass, her lips tight in self-disdain.

Legs planted firmly, Oliver stood before her. "Leslie, I want to tell you—"

She gave a violent shake of her head. "Please, no excuses."

"But there's something you should know."

Refusing to look at him, she continued to shake her head. "It must have been the moon. I don't usually forget that easily."

Embroiled in his own quandary, he swallowed more brandy, then stalked to the window. "This whole thing was crazy from the start. I can't escape it! Damn it, I can't escape it!"

"What happened just now was nothing more than sheer physical need," Leslie ranted on, no more hearing Oliver's words than he did hers. She lowered her head and put two fingers to her brow. "I can't believe I let that happen. I thought I'd learned. It was dumb. Really dumb!"

"All game playing—here, back there," Oliver growled. "I thought I could get away from it but I'm only in deeper." Whirling around, he stepped quickly forward. "Leslie...."

She sat with one hand over her face, helpless to stop the tears that flowed. Legs tucked beneath her, body curled into itself, she was unhappiness personified.

"Oh, Leslie," he groaned from somewhere deep in his throat. Within seconds he knelt before her, gently releasing the snifter from her fingers and setting the glass down on the floor. Immediately she added her other hand to her defense. "Don't cry, sweetheart." He tried to pull her hands from her face but she fought that further exposure.

"I don't cry. What's wrong with me?" she whimpered between shuddering gasps.

Oliver slid his arm across her back and drew her forward. "I don't know that, sweetheart. You'll have to tell me." He curved his fingers around her neck, twining his long fingers through her hair. "Talk to me, Les. Tell me what you feel."

"I feel . . . I feel . . . very confused. . . ."

"About us?" he whispered.

"About . . . everything. . . ." When she dissolved into another bout of quiet sobbing, he pulled her down beside him on the floor, holding her close. With his back braced against the chair, he rocked her gently, stroking her arm and the silk of her hair as he let her cry herself out.

At long last she sniffled and grew quiet. "I'm sorry," she hazarded a shaky whisper. "Now I've made your . . . shirt wet."

"It'll dry. Do you feel any better?"

She nodded, sniffling again. "I don't usually do things like this."

"We all need the outlet every once in a while," he crooned, only then looking down to wipe the tears from her cheek. "Feel like talking?"

She thought about it for a long time, hiccoughing every now and then, blotting her lower lids with the fingers of one hand. Finally she looked up at him. "I don't think I can," she whispered.

"You can tell me anything. . . ."

But she shook her head against the warmth of his chest. "I can't tell you something I don't know myself."

"You can tell me your thoughts."

"They're all jumbled up."

"Maybe I can help unjumble them."

Again she shook her head. Somehow, with the expenditure of tears, she'd purged herself of much of her tension. Now she felt . . . tired. "It's something I've got to work out, I guess."

"You're sure?"

With a sad smile, she nodded, then caught her breath. "But—Oliver?"

He smiled down. "Yes?"

"Can we sit here...like this for a little while? Just... sit here?"

He lowered his cheek to her head and gave her a tight squeeze. "Sure thing, Les. I'd like that."

They said no more for a time. Leslie nestled against him, finding quiet solace in the support of his arms, reassurance in the beat of his heart near her ear. Though her thoughts were indeed a jumble, she made no effort to unscramble them. There was too much to be savored in the utter simplicity of the moment. Just Oliver and Leslie. No past or future. Just...now.

Slowly her limbs began to slacken, and her breathing grew soft and even. Relaxation was a blissful thing, she mused as she snuggled closer to Oliver's warmth. Closing her eyes, she took a long, deep breath. Then something struck her.

"Oliver?"

"Hmmmm?" His eyes, too, were closed, his limbs at rest.

She tipped her head up. "Oliver?"

He opened his eyes. "What, sweet?"

"I still can't smell it."

"Smell what?"

"Your Homme Premier."

"I don't wear it."

"You don't wear it? Ever?"

"Ever."

"Isn't that against the laws of advertising or something?"

He hugged her more tightly and closed his eyes again. "I thought you were going to sleep."

"I think I was...then I thought of that."

"Don't like the way I smell?" he mumbled.

"I *love* the way you smell," she murmured, burrowing against his chest. "All warm and fresh and . . . manly. . . ." As though to make her point, she took a deep, long breath and sighed. "Mmmmmm. So very . . . you. . . ."

"I hope so," Oliver whispered, hugging her a final time before settling his head atop hers.

Leslie's next conscious thoughts were of the sun, the living room carpet beneath her cheek, the stiffness of limbs that had spent the night on the floor . . . and Oliver's hand on her rump.

5

IT WAS THE LAST that brought her fully awake. Squirming to a sitting position, she watched as that hand slid from her hip to the floor. Oliver was dead to the world. His tall form was sprawled prone on the rug with head turned away, his breathing slow and deep.

Stretching first one way, then the other, Leslie winced, then struggled to her feet. Her skirt and blouse were badly wrinkled, but then she'd spent the night in them. Putting a hand to her head, she tried to recall what had happened. Inevitably, her gaze returned to Oliver, and it all came back.

With sad eyes she studied his passive form. She was half in love with him, she supposed. Half in love with a man who prized his freedom, who resented being tied down for more than a day, who was no doubt the heart-throb of millions of women in America. It was a sad state of affairs.

Distractedly she made her way to the kitchen and up the stairs, finally sinking down on her bed. What other ads had he made? For what products? Wearing...what?

She knew the course of those ads. Not only would they appear in *Man's Mode*, *G.Q.* and *Esquire*, they'd appear in *Vogue* and *Cosmopolitan* as well, plus a myriad of lesser publications. His face, his body would be seen and savored by so very many eyes. In turn, he'd have his choice of the most exquisite of those admirers. Why, then, of all the places on God's green earth, was he here? And why, oh, why was he leading her on?

Rolling to her back, she stared wide-eyed at the ceiling. After all, what could he see in her? There was nothing slick or glittery about her; she'd made sure of that. Nor, despite what he'd said about her breasts, did she have a body to attract a man of his stature. So he wasn't a gigolo, as she'd originally thought. Still, he was the image of glamour, the striking playboy, the model. She, on the other hand, had chosen a different track to follow, a more quiet, private one. And she couldn't switch from it . . . any more than he could from his.

Realizing that no amount of deliberation could alter the facts, she dragged herself from the bed, showered and pulled on a clean sundress, then set out to grocery shop in Gustavia. By the time she returned to the villa, Oliver was on the beach. For a long time she stood on the terrace, unobserved, watching him. He lay absolutely still, a unified mass of bronze flesh broken only by the thin navy swatch at his hips. He loved nudity, he'd told her once. She'd love to see him strip. . . .

Frustrated by the single-mindedness of her thoughts, she whirled away, made herself a tall glass of iced tea, picked up her book and settled in a lounge on the terrace. It wasn't that she wanted to see Oliver when he left the beach, she told herself, simply that she felt like sitting on the terrace. This was, after all, her house. . . .

By a quirk of fate she dozed off. When she came to, it was with a start. Disoriented at first, she stretched and looked around, then jumped again on encountering Oliver's worried brown eyes.

"Oliver! You frightened me!"

Perched near her legs on the edge of the lounge, he smiled sadly. "We seem to have a way of doing that to each other. Are you all right?"

"I'm fine." Her hand went automatically to her wrist and, finding it bare, she frowned. "What time is it?"

"I'm not sure." He squinted upward. "I think about

one." Then his gaze returned intently to hers. "*Are* you all right?"

The deeper meaning to his question didn't escape her this time around. Slowly beginning to relax, she offered a soft and helpless smile. "I think so."

Reaching out to take her hand in his, he made study of her small, slender fingers. "About last night, Leslie—"

On elusive butterfly wings, those very fingers slipped from his and touched his lips. "Shh, Oliver. Please. Don't say anything." Her smile grew pleading. "It's not necessary. Really it's not. I think we both got . . . carried away by—" she rolled her eyes to the palms overhead "—the atmosphere of this place. There's no harm done."

"I know, but still, there's so much I want—"

"Please," she interrupted more urgently. "Please don't. Things are . . . nice just as they've been. Why upset the apple cart?"

His chuckle was harsh. "To get to the rotten apple?" he mumbled, thinned his lips in frustration and shook his head. Then he, too, raised his eyes to the palms. "The atmosphere of this place—such a simple explanation. . . ."

"If there are others," she stated soberly, "I don't want to hear them." The last thing she wanted was glib words of excuse, or worse, of affection. It was obvious that Oliver Ames had one way or another gotten himself into an uncomfortable situation. She was simply trying to offer him an easy out. "Nothing's happened here that I haven't wanted to happen. I have no regrets."

"None?" he asked, his voice a bit too low his eyes too dark.

She had the good sense to look away. "Well . . . none that can't be remedied." When she faced him again, her smile was forced. "Anyway, it's already Wednesday. I've got no intention of living with regrets for the rest of

the week. Before I know it I'll be back in New York."
Her voice cracked. "Let's not spoil things by analyzing
them to death. Okay?"

A strange look appeared on his face, and he grew
even more intense. His dark eyes held hers relent-
lessly, delving deep, finding secret paths to her soul,
leaving her raw and exposed. She felt as though she'd
been taken apart piece by piece and thoroughly pos-
sessed. When her heart beat faster, his gaze fell to her
breast.

"Oliver?" she whispered. "Okay?" Her sense of
bravado was a bygone thing.

Slowly his eyes returned to hers. "It's okay, Les. I see
your point." Patting her knee, he stood up. "I'd better
get dressed if I'm going to bike downtown."

"Take the car if you'd like. I won't be using it."

"No, thanks. I think I prefer the bike. Don't dare ride
one at home." He threw her a cynical smile. "Wouldn't
want to risk damaging the goods. The camera doesn't
take kindly to gross blemishes."

He'd left before she decided just whom he'd been
mocking—the camera, himself or her. But it didn't matter. Nothing did. As she'd told him, there was no point
in endless analysis. And before long she would be back
in New York. Strangely, this thought disturbed her
more than any other.

Alone on the beach that afternoon, with the knowledge that Oliver was in town, she yielded to impulse
and stripped off her bikini top. Her tan was really coming along, she mused, as she studied its golden hue while
spreading lotion liberally over her skin. Would anyone
see it? Not on her breasts. No one but herself—and she'd
remember.... And grow warm just thinking about lying on the beach—beside Oliver.

It was a lovely memory, even if it had nowhere to go.
Where were they now? Back to square one, each going

his own way, leaving the other in peace. Funny how "peace" could take on such different meanings. . . .

FOR LESLIE, a special kind of peace came that evening when, out of the blue, Oliver appeared at the door of the den. "Hi, Les."

She looked up with barely suppressed pleasure at the sight of the tall, casually lounging figure. "Hi."

"Whatcha doin'?"

"Crossword puzzle." She slapped her pencil against it. "Lousy puzzle. I'm really stuck."

"Need some help?"

"Oh, no." She held up a hand and pressed the paper to her chest. "I can do it. It may take me several days, but I'll get it if it kills me."

"You like word games?"

Most likely they bored him to tears. "I do," she said pertly, tipping her chin up in challenge. Wearing cutoffs and a open short-sleeved shirt, Oliver looked disgustingly virile. She needed something to dilute the effect of him; a challenge was just the thing.

"Are you any good?" he asked, eyes shining.

Leslie gave a modest shrug. "I've never won any championships, but I think I can hold my own."

"Got Scrabble?"

"Uh huh."

He tipped his head almost shyly. "Are you game?"

"Are *you*?" she countered in surprise.

"Sure."

They played Scrabble until midnight, broke for several rounds of Boggle and some coffee, then returned to the Scrabble board. Whether it was the lateness of the hour or the pleasure of being with Oliver, Leslie didn't know. But when, sometime around two, giddiness set in and the choice of words took a decidedly suggestive turn, she played right along. After all, it was a game only a game.

SOFT. SENSUAL. LIBIDO.

"Good one, Oliver!"

BED.

"Come on, Les. You can do better than that."

"I'm trying. But I haven't got any vowels."

"Here. Let me give you a couple."

VIRILE.

"Very smooth."

CARESS.

"Not bad. I thought you didn't have any vowels."

"I just picked them. Go on. Your turn."

WARMTH. FLOW. WAIF.

"Thirty points, Oliver. You're good at this."

SPA. SIR. KEYS.

"Pure, Leslie. Very pure."

SEX.

"Oliver! That's a nothing word!"

"I wouldn't say that. It's got an x. That's worth eight points."

"But you didn't even get it on a double or triple score. You blew it."

"I'll say," he muttered under his breath. "Your turn."

AROUSE. GROAN. RAPE. BREAST.

"I don't know, Ol. This is getting pretty bawdy. Hey, you can't use *breast*. You've got two blanks in there that aren't really blanks. The other two are already on the board. That's cheating."

"Come on, Les. Where's your sense of humor? *Breast* is a great word!"

"It's bawdy. Try again."

BAWDY.

"That's not fair. I gave it to you."

"Uh uh, Les. You didn't have the letters. I don't like that gleam in your eye."

"Hold onto your socks. *Bawdy* is nothing. Look at this."

QUIVER.

"Triple word score, plus double letter on the *v*. Twelve...twenty...twenty-two...that makes sixty-six points. So you can keep *bawdy*, even though the *y* does run off the board."

For the moment she'd taken the upper hand. Then, in the last move of the game, Oliver struck.

LOVE.

No double or triple word score. Not even a double or triple letter score for the *v*. Nothing but the emotional clout of a simple four-letter word.

Strangely and mutually subdued, they called it a night after that.

DESPITE ITS POIGNANT ENDING, the camaraderie they shared that Wednesday night carried over to Thursday. By silent agreement they spent the day together, starting with Leslie's mushroom omelets for breakfast, moving down to the beach for several hours of sun and surf, finally doubling up on the motorbike for a shopping expedition into Gustavia.

"You're sure you're up for this?" Oliver asked, strapping a helmet on her head before donning his own.

"Of course. I've taken the bike out myself many times."

"The roads are narrow."

"I'll hang on tight. Hey, are you sure *you're* up for it?"

Taking in her knowing grin, he returned with a pointed stare. "I will be soon," he growled, tossing his leg over the bike, reaching an arm back to settle her snugly behind him, then setting off.

To Leslie, nothing could have been more exhilarating. Wearing shorts and a T-shirt, she felt the sun's rays in counterpoint to the breeze whipping her skin. And Oliver—so firm and hard and strong between her thighs, against her stomach and her breasts— She held on for dear life, her arms wrapped around his lean middle, her hands flattened on his ribs.

"Okay?" he called back once, rubbing her hand with one of his own in a warmly endearing gesture.

"You bet," she returned, closing her eyes as she pressed her cheek to his back. To have a viable excuse to do this was...was ecstasy.

To her delight, the ecstasy continued long after they left the bike at the quai and began to stroll along the streets. Oliver kept her hand tucked firmly in his, holding her close to his side as they ambled idly in and out of shops in search of nothing in particular. Indeed, they chanced upon a kind of euphoria; they were a couple among many couples, yet were oblivious to all but each other.

Twice, as they browsed, they stopped at small cafés to sit and talk and further savor the atmosphere of the town. The few purchases they made were Leslie's—a bottle of imported perfume, a small enameled box and, on a whim, a soft pink pareo made of an original hand-blocked fabric that had appealed to her instantly. She knew that the three items would have special meaning for her, given the circumstances under which they'd been bought. Her only regret was that the bag holding them came between Oliver and herself during the airy ride back to the villa.

"How about a swim?" Oliver asked as he parked the bike next to the car.

Leslie smiled and stretched. "I don't know. I feel really lazy. I think I could go to sleep. What with late nights and fresh air and walking...."

"Come down to the beach with me, then. You can sleep while I swim."

To her amazement, that was precisely what she did. She remembered seeing Oliver dive into the waves, watching him swim for a minute...then nothing. Once she stirred, finding the warm body near her in her sleep and snuggling closer. When she awoke, Oliver was there, sleeping beside her, his arms cradling her ever so gently. Turning carefully, she raised her head and looked at him. His face was the image of peacefulness. In turn, her own glowed.

"Oliver?" she breathed in a whisper.

"Mmmmmm?" He didn't move.

"You awake?"

"Sure," he murmured in a sleep-slurred voice. "Just have my eyes closed."

"Is that all?" she teased.

"Sure. Late nights don't bother me. Do it all the time." He smacked his lips lightly together once, twice, then his head lolled to the side. His eyes still hadn't opened.

Capitalizing on a rare opportunity, Leslie made a free study of his chest. She loved the smoothness of his skin with its soft mat of hair. She loved the way his nipples hid amid dark whorls of chest hair, camouflaged in apt reminder of a dormant sexuality. She admired the fluid span of his collarbone and the way the muscles of his shoulder had bunched to accommodate her head. She was fascinated by the more vulnerable skin on the underside of his arm and the silkiness of hair there. She raised her fingers to touch, momentarily resisted the temptation, then yielded.

"Hey!" Oliver came alive at once, capturing her hand with unerring aim. "That tickles!" One eye opened, deep and brown. "You must be bored."

"Oh, no."

"Restless?"

"A little."

"Hungry?"

"Mmm."

The double-entendre sizzled between them for a breathtaking minute. Then Oliver snatched her to him and hugged her tight. "My God, Les!" he exclaimed softly as he crushed her to his bare skin. She felt the tremor of his arms and knew an elementary satisfaction that was in no way lessened when he set her back.

"Let's clean up and go into town for dinner," he suggested in a deep voice. "I'm in the mood for something. . . hot and spicy."

"Creole? That's funny. I would have thought you'd prefer soft and subtle and classic."

The sudden smokiness of his gaze sent corresponding spirals smoldering through her. "Later," he crooned. "Later."

It was a promise that was foremost on Leslie's mind. When she bathed, it was with special care to leave her skin soft and aromatic. When she styled her hair, it was with attention to even the smallest wisps. When she made herself up, it was with the lightest hand, no more than the most subtle emphasis on eyes and cheekbones.

Come time to dress, there was no question of her choice. Padding from the bathroom into the bedroom wrapped in a towel, she took the exquisite pink pareo from its bag, shook it out, studied its gentle floral print for a minute, then turned to the mirror. Loosening the terry knot at her breast, she let the towel fall to the floor. Her eye slid from her naked body to the print, then back. With careful concentration, she straightened the fabric, held it up to herself and began to wrap it around the pliant lines of her body, finally criss-crossing the ends at the hollow of her throat and tying a loose knot at the back of her neck.

Then she turned to study herself. It was perfect. Had she picked it out with this in mind? She ran her hands down along her hips, eminently aware of the smooth, unbroken line. Soft pink. Just as the Homme Premier sculptor had requested. Soft pink. Just for Oliver.

When he met her at the front door at eight, he was very obviously affected. For a minute he simply looked at her, devouring every soft inch, every gentle curve. "You look...beautiful, Leslie. Absolutely beautiful."

She felt it. She felt beautiful. She felt...special. In spite of all their many differences, in spite of the more glossy women he'd surely known in his time, in spite of all the power and grace and raw virility that the man exuded in his fine-tailored slacks and designer shirt, he had a way of making her feel as though there had never been, as though there never would be, another woman for him.

Leslie barely knew what she ate that night, only that she sat at an intimate table for two, elbow to elbow with Oliver, and that he didn't take his eyes from her the entire time. They may have talked of interesting things, but conversation, too, was secondary to mood. Had she tried to classify it she would have used words like loving, needing and expectant. For those feelings permeated her being, blinding her to everything but Oliver.

Somehow, sitting there at a small table in an unpretentious restaurant on the warm, cozy island of St. Barts, she was ready to play the game she'd decried for so long. She was ready to believe that Oliver was as taken with her as she was with him, that they were positively meant for each other, that what existed between them would be right and good and lasting. What he was in real life didn't matter any more than did her own past or future. They were together now and, in the illusion, very much in love. That was all that mattered.

"Dessert?" Oliver murmured, fingers entwined with hers, eyes adoring her lips as the waiter stood nearby.

Entranced by the faint but roguish shadow of his beard, she shook her head. "No," she whispered.

"You're sure?" he whispered back, as distracted as she was.

She nodded.

Within minutes they were in the car headed back to the villa. There, Oliver led her on the long path around the house, holding her hand tightly, turning at times to circle her waist and lift her over a tricky patch of rocks. When at last they reached the beach, he took her in his arms.

It was as if she'd been waiting for just this moment all night, all week, all month, all year. Shorn of inhibition by the aura of love surrounding them, she stood on tiptoe and wrapped her arms around his neck. When her feet left the ground completely and he gently rocked her back and forth, she hung on all the more tightly.

"Ahh, Leslie, this is what I've wanted." Setting her feet back on the ground, he curved his body over hers and buried his lips against her neck. His arms crushed her to him with a fierceness that in itself thrilled her as much as did the feel of his long, lean lines. "So beautiful. . . ."

"Like you," she whispered as she ran her fingers through his hair. Inclining her face, she buried it in that vibrant shock. His scent was clean and rich, pure and unadulterated by fragrant colognes or balms. Breathing deeply, she was further intoxicated. It was only his straightening that brought her away.

His eyes were hot and intense, echoing the silver light of the moon as it shimmied over the waves. He raised a hand to her cheek, tracing its sculpted line, the curve of her jaw, her ear. "I want to kiss you, Les," he rasped. "I want to kiss you everywhere."

If his words hadn't sent fire through her veins, his restless hands would have done the trick. Straining closer, Leslie tilted up her mouth in sweet invitation, then gave him everything when he accepted her offer. There was no teasing, no feint and parry, but rather an all-out meeting of minds, of hearts, of bodies.

Her lips parted before his thirsty advance, moving with and against him just as anxiously. When his tongue plunged inward, she opened to receive him and suck him deeper. She needed to know of his hunger, absolutely loved the feel of his consuming her, indeed wanted him to know every dark niche within.

All the while, his hands charted the outer landscape of her femininity, sliding around and across her back, over the gentle swell of her hips, the firm contour of her bottom. He lifted her, pressed her more closely, set her down and began again.

Deep within, a gathering of fire had begun. Never before in her life had Leslie known such an intensity of need. But then, Oliver's body was perfect. Arching against him, she felt its every contour. Her hands scoured him, mapping the breadth of his shoulders, the tapering length of his torso, the slimness of his hips, the solidity of his thighs. Around the latter her fingers splayed, sliding up and down as the sinewed cords beneath his slacks grew more taut. She felt the tremor that buzzed through him and found satisfaction that she could have caused it. But her satisfaction was quickly burned to a crisp beneath the flame of a hunger that flashed through her own limbs. When Oliver's voice came, thick and low by her ear, she quivered all over.

"You're not wearing anything under this, are you?"

He drew back only to see her face. In the moonlight it had a pale silver glow and looked all the more fragile.

"No," she whispered, eyes strangely innocent.

"For me?"

She shrugged shyly. "I wanted to feel . . . sexy. I did."

"Do you now?"

"Oh, yes," she breathed.

"And . . . if I took the pareo off, would you still?"

Her pulse had taken such a giant leap that she could only nod. It was what she wanted, what her entire body craved. Somehow hearing his intent was all the more erotic. She reached back to the knot at her neck, only to have his warm hands pull her arms away.

"Let me," he murmured, dipping his head to kiss her slowly, languorously, before turning his attention to the knot. His eyes held hers while his fingers worked, gently pulling at the ends of the cloth, steadily loosening them.

When she felt the fabric slacken at her chest, Leslie felt a moment's hesitation. There was nothing at all glamorous about her body. And though he'd seen most of it already, there was something very . . . special about that part he'd now see for the first time. But it was too late to go back, she knew. If the determined look on Oliver's face hadn't told her so, the soft tendrils of excitement skittering in the pit of her stomach would have.

Slowly he drew his hands forward, unwinding the fabric and letting it fall to the sand. As though sensing her need for support, he instantly put his hands on her shoulders, rubbing them gently as his eyes fell to delight in her.

"Oh . . . Les . . ." he managed brokenly.

She caught in her breath. "Is it . . . am I . . . ?"

Only then did he look back to see the unsureness on her face. While one hand tightened on her shoulder, the other slid up to her neck. "You were worried?" he asked in surprise.

"I'm not gorgeous. . . ."

Helplessly drawn by the golden sheen of her skin, his gaze fell, to journey with his hand in a slow descent. The texture of his palm was the slightest bit rough in contrast to the butter-smooth skin of her breasts. His fingers seemed that much stronger than her waist, her hips, almost able to circle her thighs. But when they feather-touched the golden curls he'd never seen before, his hands were all male and dynamite.

In response to their tender force, Leslie reached out to clutch his shoulders in support. "Oliver!" she whispered hoarsely.

"You were worried?" he repeated dumbly as his hands flowed down and around and back up. Everywhere they touched she felt ready to explode. Again she moaned his name.

Framing her face with his hands, he tipped it up to his. "You're magnificent, sweetheart. Every inch of you. So warm—" he brushed his lips to her nose "—and soft—" he licked the line of her cheekbone "—and full where you should be full, and moist just there. . . ." His lips became pulsing things then, capturing hers with a frenzy that spoke more eloquently than anything else might have done. And Leslie surrendered to their argument, giving herself up to the fire of the moment, choosing to believe she was indeed as magnificent as he'd claimed.

For a minute, held and holding breathlessly onto him, she savored the feel of his clothing against her skin. It made her feel naked and naughty and sensual. Yet when she burrowed her head against the column of his neck and opened her lips to the heat of his skin where his shirt fell open, she wanted more. Naked and naughty and sensual were very lovely narcissistic things to be. But what she felt for Oliver went far beyond narcissistic.

As she kissed the bronzed hollow of his shoulder, her hands worked feverishly at the buttons of his shirt, releasing one after the other, finally tugging the material from his pants and brushing it away. Then, with a sigh of delight, she set her hands loose on the playground of his chest, feeling as though in being able to touch him at will she'd been given the greatest gift of all.

"That's right," Oliver moaned, pressing his hands to the small of her back to keep their lower bodies close despite the inches that separated them above. "I've wanted you to touch me for so long—to feel your hands on my body...."

"Tell me what you like, Oliver," she whispered as she spread her fingers wide and ran them up his sides. When her thumbs grazed his nipples, he jerked. Returning to them, she circled their tips, tormenting them with the pads of her thumbs until he moaned again.

"Like that," he gasped, his eyes closed, his chest laboring in the effort to breathe. She found that to please him, to bring his body alive, was a joy in itself. Growing bolder, she bent her head and replaced her fingers with her lips. With the tip of her tongue she danced along his flesh, dabbing the hardened nipple with a sensual moistness, grazing it with her teeth. This time in response his groan was one of sweet agony. Crushing her bottom with his hands, he ground his hips to hers.

His voice was a low, unsteady rasp, his eyes wild with fire when he tore her head up. "I don't know how much more I can take, Leslie," he warned. "I've needed you so badly all week—and now...."

Setting her back, he attacked the buckle of his belt. It was released, along with his zipper, in an instant. But as he would have thrust the fabric down, Leslie reached out.

"Wait!" she cried, then at his stricken look realized his misconception. "No," she whispered, stepping closer, "it's just that I want to do it." Arching against him, her hands at his waist, she stretched to reach his lips. Her breasts strained against his chest, creating a heady friction that gave even greater heat to her kiss. Then, offering him her tongue by way of exchange, she slid her hands beneath the band of his briefs, sought and found what she wanted, and stroked him tenderly. Fully aroused, he was thick and hard. She found herself breathing as heavily as he was, needing to touch him, yet needing so much more.

Oliver moaned again, and a shiver shook his limbs. Setting her aside almost roughly, he thrust slacks and briefs down over his legs and cast them aside, then caught her again.

At the contact, she cried aloud. It was new, rich and electric.

"Oh, Les...."

"Yes, yes...."

"Come here!" The last was a command ground out from his chest moments before he slid his hands down the backs of her thighs and lifted her, spreading her legs, fitting them snugly around his hips. Then, poised on the brink of her, he dropped smoothly to his knees and gently lowered her backward. Only when she was fully cushioned by the sand did he retrieve his hands. With one he propped himself up, with the other he reached down to unerringly find her warmth.

"Please, Oliver..." she pleaded, moving against his hand in frustration.

"Do you want me?"

"Oh, yes!"

His fingers caressed her longingly. "You're ready...."

"I've been ready for so long—I don't think I can stand much more. . . ."

"I can't," he grated hoarsely. Planting his other hand near her shoulder, he moved his hips against hers.

They looked into each other's eyes then, aware of the moment as of no other before. To Leslie, it was right—right in every way, form and fashion. Not only did her body want Oliver, but her mind and her heart did as well. Regrets would be nonexistent, regardless of what the future held. For the moment to come promised to be the culmination of something very special to her as a woman. Pulse racing in wild anticipation, she grasped his hips and urged him in.

Ever wary of hurting her, he rocked slowly, surging forward by degrees, conquering her by inches. Her mouth opened in silent exclamation at the beauty of it, the slow filling, the exquisite heat. When at last he was fully buried within her, he dropped his head back and let his breath out in a soulful rush.

"You have no idea, Leslie. . . ."

"But I do," she cried, lifting her hips and hooking her ankles together at his waist. "I do," she breathed, tightening herself, closing her eyes with the sweet, sweet pleasure of knowing that Oliver was deep inside.

On arms that trembled, he lowered his head to envelop her mouth. Then he began to move his hips, slowly at first but with growing speed and power as the flight of passion caught him up.

Leslie was with him every step of the way. Her lips answered his hungry nips, her hands roamed in greedy caress through the damp sheen of sweat rising on his skin. She felt his strength and the rock-hard boldness moving within her and, coaxed by instinct, caught the rhythm of his fire.

In those instants what existed between them was raw and primal and devoid of identity other than that of an all-consuming and mutual need. Labels would have been useless; Oliver was no more the glamorous male model than she the private preschool teacher. The pleasure they brought each other was direct and intense, unsullied by anything either of them might have been or done or wanted before in their lives. There were just the two of them, making love at that moment; nothing else was of consequence.

"Oliver!" she cried from a daze of passion, her body alive with a fire frightening in its intensity.

"That's it, sweet," he urged, plunging ever deeper, "more...oh, yes...there...."

She cried his name again, strained upward, then dissolved into spasms of ecstasy. In the next instant Oliver, too, stiffened, then let out an anguished moan of joy as his pleasure went endlessly on.

At last, totally spent, he collapsed over her. Then, when her gasping grew as loud as his, he quickly levered himself up on his elbows to relieve her of the worst of his weight. His gaze its most tender, he looked down at her.

"Does that smile mean that you're happy?"

Her throat felt suspiciously tight. She nodded.

"I'm glad," he said softly, brushing his lips against a corner of the smile in question. "You are beautiful. That was beautiful." He paused for a breath between each brief burst of words, then slowly slipped to her side, leaving one thigh firmly over hers. "Well, what do you think?" His tone verged on the giddy, yet she knew that deep down he needed to know that he'd pleased her. She also knew that it had very little to do with ego, and she was enchanted.

She brushed the dark wave from the dampness of his brow, then repeated the gesture when it fell right back down again. "I think," she began with mock deliberation, "that for a professional ladykiller you do just fine."

"I'm glad," he murmured, "because if my past has been worth anything, it's been to make me better for you."

"That's a sweet thing to say."

"It's what I feel, Leslie." He was suddenly serious. "You do know that it's never been like that before, don't you?"

Because she wanted to believe him, she nodded.

"You also know that I'm now very sandy."

"You ain't the only one." Before she could say another word, Oliver was on his feet, dragging her up with him. "What are you doing?" she cried, then pulled back on her hand. "Oh, no, Oliver Ames, it's chilly in there this time of night! You're not getting *me* in there."

"It's only the air that's chilly," he chided, dealing with her resistance by sweeping her into his arms.

"Oliver! You're supposed to be limp and sleepy. You can't do this!"

"I'm doin' it." His feet were making definite tracks, and not toward the house.

"But, Oliver!" She held tightly to his neck when she heard the splashing at his feet. "Oliver!" He bounced farther into the waves. "Come on, Oliver!" When the water touched her bottom, she strained upward, only to slide helplessly down when he released her legs.

Even the placid light of the moon couldn't hide the mischief in his eyes. His hands went to his neck. "Let go of me, Leslie," he murmured silkily.

She shook her head and locked her hands all the more tightly. "No."

He spread his hands beneath her arms. "Let go . . . ."

"No."

Then he tickled her. On a reflex of self-defense, she lowered her arms . . . and tumbled helplessly into the waves. Never once did he totally release her, though.

His hands were there at her waist to lift her as soon as she'd been fully submerged.

"That was a dirty trick!" she sputtered. Tossing her wet hair back from her face, she scowled, but he pulled her against him once more and she melted nearly on contact.

"Now you can hold on again."

"Uh uh. You'll only tickle again."

"I promise I won't."

"Yeah, yeah."

"Really."

She wanted to believe. "Really?"

"Uh huh."

She hesitated for only a moment longer. Then, sensual slave that she happily was, she locked her arms around his neck once more. The fit of their bodies was perfect. "Only problem is that you've still got sand on you, and now it's back on me."

"Oh?" He frowned, as though stymied by the problem. Then, with an innocent shrug, he twirled and fell backward into the sea, dunking them both.

This time she came up laughing. When Oliver grasped her around the waist and hoisted her higher against him, she looked adoringly down at him. "That was nearly as dirty a trick as the other."

"But we're clean," he murmured between nips at her chin, "aren't we?"

Her legs floated around him naturally. "Uh huh."

"Are you too cool?"

"In your arms? Never."

He tipped her back and looked at her then. The moonlight set his features in relief, giving them a masterful air in counterpoint to the tenderness of his voice. "Why is it that you've always got the right answers?"

"They're not necessarily right," she replied lightly, "just honest."

"You like honesty?"

"I need honesty."

"Spoken with the same vehemence I've heard from you more than once before." He paused. "What happened, Leslie?"

Her legs slipped slowly downward. "What do you mean?"

"You've been hurt. Something happened. I want to know."

"You don't really," she said, trying to make light of it.

"I do." His expression echoed his words. "I want to understand why you feel so strongly about some things. Why you put that certain distance between you and your family. Why you seem leery of men."

"I don't know, Oliver. It's really irrelevant...and very embarrassing." He would think her a positive fool!

"Then—" he swept her up in his arms, turned and started for shore "—you'd better talk quickly so that the darkness can hide your blush. I intend to hear about it...tonight!"

"Or...?" Her arms were around his neck once more.

"Or else."

"Or else what?"

"Or else...I'll hold you prisoner, stake you spread-eagled out in the sun tomorrow morning, and let you fry until you talk."

"Mmm, sounds very provocative."

Out of the water now, he stopped dead in his tracks. "Primitive is the word."

She gave a playful growl. "Primitive turns me on."

"Leslie, you're not being serious—but you won't get away with it." He let her feet fall to the sand, holding her waist until he was sure she had her balance. "Now pick up your things, and let's get up to the house. We've got some talking to do."

She picked up her sandals and let them dangle from one hand. "Oliver?"

He was searching the night sand for a second sock, his body lean and glistening in the moonlight. "Mmm?"

Inching closer, she wrapped an arm around his waist. His skin felt slick and smooth; her flesh slid easily over it. "Wouldn't you rather make love?" she asked softly, her expression more heartfelt than seductive.

He popped a kiss on the tip of her nose. "That, sweet angel, will be your reward. Now up!"

6

ACTUALLY, they didn't make it beyond the upper terrace. Stubbing her toe on the corner of a lounge chair she hadn't seen in the dark, Leslie needed consolation. Much later Oliver was to tell her that she'd simply wanted to make love on every level. But he hadn't complained at the time. Rather, there had been a kind of poignant drive to his lovemaking that had surprised her, given the satisfaction they'd so recently found on the beach. It was almost as though he feared what he'd learn when they talked.

He wasn't deterred, however. After they'd reached Shangri-la and beyond, had lain savoring the sensations, then recovered enough to languidly leave the lounge and pick up their clothes once more, he ushered her into the den. He left her only to go in search of robes, returned to gently clothe them both, then folded his long frame into the chair opposite hers and leaned forward.

She simply stared at him.

"Okay, Les," he began, undaunted. "Let's have it."

"Aren't you exhausted?"

"Nope. Who was he?"

Leslie tucked her legs beneath her and wrapped her arms around her middle. "It's not important."

"I think it is."

"It's *my* past. I don't ask you about yours."

He took on the same mocking expression she'd seen more than once before. "That's because mine is so lurid and filled with such an endless stream of women that I wouldn't know where to begin."

"Well," she prevaricated, "maybe mine's the same. Maybe I have a hidden past. Maybe I'm not as pure as I let on."

He chuckled and sat back, momentarily indulging her. "Funny, I never thought of you simply as 'pure.' Maybe pure honey or pure wit or pure sensuality. Never just...'pure.' Besides—" he came forward again, his dark eyes narrowed "—you were the one who informed me—albeit in a very sexy voice—that you didn't sleep around."

She recalled the moment exactly, the Friday before, when she'd first arrived from New York and had been sick and very threatened by his presence. How far she'd come, she mused, then abruptly realized she hadn't. If she stopped to think, she'd know that she was still very threatened indeed, though by something quite different now.

"So, Les," Oliver went on, reaching forward to brush his thumb against the furrows on her brow, "tell me about it." His voice was quiet, patient. "Tell me about honesty. Too many times I've heard bitterness, then just now vehemence, in your voice when you've mentioned it. You need it, you say. Why?"

Quiet and patient, yes. But there was also an unmistakable trace of cynicism underlying his tone. Disturbed, Leslie tore her gaze away. "It's not relevant to anything, Oliver."

Though his stance remained casual, long bare legs set nonchalantly, hands now crossed over his stomach, his gaze was sharp. "It's relevant to us...and to what's happened twice now. And it matters to me. I need to understand you."

It was the last that hit home. She mulled the words over again and again. *I need to understand you...need to understand you.* Perhaps it was nothing more than a continuation of the illusion born earlier that day and brought to fulfillment on the beach. But she wanted so badly to believe that he cared that at long last she yielded and spoke, softly, slowly, eyes downcast, arms clutched tightly about herself.

"It's really very simple," she began. "I grew up a Parish, always a Parish. Living in an exclusive area, going to a private school, my friends were pretty much . . . people like me, people wh'd had most everything they'd wanted in life." She lifted her eyes to find Oliver sitting back, listening thoughtfully. "Oh, I had friends. A couple of good ones I've kept. But at some point I became disillusioned with most of them. They seemed shallow. Boring. Quick to manipulate when it suited their purposes. Maybe it was natural for me to rebel. I was the youngest Parish and felt I had gone through life in the shadow of the others. I was seventeen and feeling my oats. Having always had the material things I'd wanted and knowing that they'd always be there for me, it was easy to turn my back on them."

"You became a flower child?" Oliver asked, faint amusement lighting his features.

She blushed. "Not really. Just a free thinker. I did little things to proclaim my individuality—like going vegetarian and boycotting the senior prom and donating my graduation money to Oxfam and biking across the country with three friends."

Again his eyes lit. "Bicycling?"

She lowered hers. "Motorcycling."

"And the three other kids?" he asked more pointedly.

"My best friend from school . . . and her twin cousins."

He caught the drop in her voice and interpreted correctly. "Male?"

"Yes." She raised a defensive gaze and went quickly

on. "Not that anything happened between us. I mean, we were all good friends, but that was it. We didn't cause trouble, either. Our idea of adventure was in living as cheaply as we could. We camped out a good part of the time, stayed in our share of sleazy places. Just knowing how appalled our parents would have been enhanced our joy." She sighed. "We did see the country, I have to admit." Then she qualified the statement. "I mean, we'd all seen the country before, but never like that."

"Sounds like fun," Oliver ventured wryly.

"It was! It really was. We enjoyed mocking everything we'd always had. Then the other three went right back to it when the summer was over."

"And you?"

"I went on to college. Berkeley." When he winced, she smiled. "It wasn't so bad. Actually, I'd already gotten much of the rebelliousness out of my system, so I was pretty receptive to learning. I felt confident and in control and loved the idea of being three thousand miles away from all of the other Parishes."

"They didn't keep close tabs on you?"

"Naw. They trusted me."

He arched a brow. "Should they have?"

She thought for a minute, then nodded. "My intentions were good. I was idealistic, bent on making a very serious, independent way in the world. I would never have done anything to disgrace them." She paused, then frowned. "Not knowingly, at least."

Silence sat between them for a time, broken only by the gentle murmur of the night surf on the beach as it accompanied the softest of breezes through the open glass doors. Leslie let herself be momentarily lulled, then, eager to get out the worst, she went on.

"I had a great freshman year. I loved school and did well." She cast him a sheepish look. "It was an awakening to find myself among so many people who were legitimately serious and independent. In many ways, it was humbling. I guess I withdrew a little, letting the place itself speak for my rebellion while I got reacquainted with the person I was inside. I liked myself. I thought I'd found a nice blend between 'way out' and 'way in'...." Her voice trailed off as her eyes reflected a distant pain.

"Then what happened?"

As though she'd forgotten his presence, she came back with a start. With a shrug she looked down at the pleats her fingers were nervously folding into the terry fabric of her robe. "I met a fellow. A med student." She tossed her head to the side, keeping her eyes downcast, safe from Oliver's intent study. "He was tall and good-looking and bright and funny...and very high on life and himself." Her voice took on a gently mocking tone. "He was going to be a doctor. You know, heal the world?"

"I know the type," Oliver injected, but Leslie was too immersed in her story to hear the dryness in his tone.

"Anyway," she sighed, "we started to date and... things got pretty heavy. We couldn't see each other often. I was busy studying, and his schedule was ten times worse. I think it was the time we spent apart that aided his cause more than anything. I was young and starry-eyed and spent those times away from him imagining all the wonderful things he was going to do." She lowered her voice to a self-conscious murmur, "All the wonderful things we were going to do together. He was talking about the Peace Corps. That fit right into my scheme of things—noble, stoic, commendable. I spent those days alone dreaming about how, after graduation, we'd both go to South America or South Africa. He'd doctor; I'd teach. It was perfect." She paused to recall that particular illusion, then shook her head in dismay. "Things didn't quite work out as as I'd dreamed."

Oliver propped his elbows on his knees and prodded gently. "Why not?"

She looked up then, vulnerable and in pain. "He was married."

"Oh. And you didn't know."

"Of course not!" she cried, doubly hurt. "I'd never have knowingly had an affair with a married man! For all my ballyhooing about rebellion, I'd been pretty conservative about sex; it was enough for me to have had the affair in the first place! I honestly thought that he was busy studying all the time. I mean—" again the mocking tone "—between classes and rotations, a med student has to be the most put-upon person in the world. Hmmph," she mused aloud, "no wonder they go out into the world and keep patients in their offices waiting for hours. Revenge, I'm sure. Simple revenge."

Oliver let her anger gradually seep away before he spoke. "Not all doctors are that way, Les. There are ones who do serve time in the Peace Corps, or who keep ungodly hours as staff physicians well after their med-school days are over, or who go into private practice and make a point to see all their patients on time. How they are as doctors can sometimes be very different from the way they run their private lives."

"I'm not so sure about that," she retorted bitterly, "though I'll concede you the point. For all I know Joe's become an excellent doctor. And for that matter, I may have been as much at fault for what happened between us as he was." At Oliver's puzzled look, she explained. "Idealistic young thing that I was, I accepted everything on faith. He explained that when he was free he wanted to get away from it all. So he always came to my place, rather than the other way around. Sucker that I was, I believed him."

"Did you love him?" came the quiet follow-up.

"What I knew of him, yes. He was truly charming—

great bedside manner, if you'll excuse the pun." Her lips thinned. "We'd been seeing each other for nearly six months when one day I thought I'd surprise him and bring a home-cooked dinner to his apartment. I knew his address in Palo Alto, though I'd never been there before." She swallowed hard, trying to accept all over again what she'd learned that day. "It was a lovely dorm not far from the medical school. Prettier than most— you know, small balconies with hanging plants and a baby swing here and there. When I went into the lobby to buzz him, I understood why. It was a married students' dorm. 'Dr. and Mrs.' all along the roster—the Joe Durands right up there with the rest. I turned around with my shattered dreams and went home."

By way of offering comfort, Oliver took her hand, but it lay limply under his gentle massage. "Did he ever follow you?"

"Oh, yes," she spat out with a harsh laugh. "He hadn't known I'd come and didn't know anything was wrong. He assumed his little game could go on indefinitely. When he showed up several days later, I'd had time to cool off and gather my thoughts. I was really quite...good."

"I'm sure," Oliver remarked tightly.

"I was," she insisted, raising her eyes in a burst of courage. "It was actually funny. I threw myself into his arms and told him how much I'd missed him, how much I loved him. After he tossed back those same hollow words, I told him about my brainstorm. It had occurred to me, I told him, that he'd be able to save all kinds of money if he moved in with me. I could cook for him and do his laundry and take care of him in between my own studies. After all, why not, since we loved each other so much?"

"That was mean," Oliver scolded, though he couldn't completely hide the glimmer of admiration in his gaze.

"It was intended to be," she rejoined without remorse. "I was brokenhearted at the time. I felt used and dirty. I had to score some points, and since I didn't have the heart to resort to blackmail, I simply wanted him to squirm."

"Did he?"

"Oh ho, yes," she answered, neither pride nor pleasure in her tone. "He hemmed and hawed about how he'd never get any studying done if we lived together, and he'd feel all the more guilty about having to put me off when he did need to work. I insisted that it wouldn't bother me and that it would be better watching him study than not seeing him at all."

The fire in her eyes spoke of an inner strength. Respecting it, Oliver grew more grave. "How did he handle that?"

"Very predictably, actually. On the pretense of being overcome by my offer, he took me in his arms and tried to put off the whole discussion by making love."

"You didn't—"

"No. I brought my knee up hard, and then told him to go home and *try* to make love to his wife."

Oliver jacked forward as though in physical pain himself. "You really did that?"

"You bet I did," she breathed, "and I haven't regretted it for a minute. I was hurt and angry. The look of surprise, then disbelief, then sheer terror on his face was the small satisfaction I got out of the affair. That . . . and the determination never to be made a fool of again." With the last of her venom trickling into thin air, she spoke more gently and with an awareness of Oliver once more. His face was racked by pain; she was touched by his sympathy. "It's okay, Oliver," she said, forcing a smile. "It's over, and I survived. In hindsight. I guess I was most disappointed in myself—disappointed that I'd been fool enough to be so completely taken in. I really did love a part of Joe. I thought I'd found someone different—someone down-to-earth, someone more concerned with doing and living than clawing up the social ladder." Her voice grew sad. "I was wrong. His greatest fear, when he discovered I knew the truth, was that I'd blow the whistle on him and somehow hurt his chances for a future in Boston. Not Kenya. Boston." She sighed, her tone a mere whisper. "Boy, was I wrong."

For the longest time, Oliver simply sat and stared at her, his chin propped on his fist, his face a mask of dismay. When she could no longer stand the silence, Leslie pushed herself from her chair and paced to the window.

"So now you know what a clever lady I am," she called over her shoulder. "Now you know why I'm wary."

With the sound of his bare feet muffled in the carpet, she didn't hear him approach. When his arms slipped around her to draw her back against him, she resisted. But he was insistent. And in the end she needed his support.

"I'm sorry," he murmured so sadly that Leslie turned in his arms to face him.

"You're sorry?" she asked, bemused by his almost anguished expression. "It wasn't your fault!"

"But still...in some ways I identify with...your Joe."

"He's not my Joe, and that's ridiculous. Aside from the fact that you both wear pants, you're nothing at all like Joe. He was a two-timing liar. You're not. You've never made promises or said things you couldn't see through. You've never made any attempt to deliberately sweeten the image of what you do, even when I've thought the worst." Her ardent claim did nothing to ease his pain.

"But you know so little about me," he began, his voice heavy and low.

"I know the essentials," she pointed out quietly. "And Tony knows you. If there was something grossly unsuitable about you, he would never have suggested you come. Besides, I know that you were kind enough not to laugh at me just now."

"Did anyone laugh?" he asked, brows lifting in a touching challenge. Was he truly a knight in shining armor, prepared to defend her virtue?

"No one laughed," she murmured, "because no one knew. And if anyone finds out," she warned only half in jest, "I'll personally knock you off that white steed of yours."

Attuned to the analogy, he grunted. "Better to fall from a horse than to be kicked in the balls. Hell, you're a dangerous woman."

"Only when I'm pushed. I don't really want to be dangerous."

Oliver's expression took a soulful twist as his arms tightened around her back. "Oh, Leslie," he murmured, his gaze clinging to each of her features in turn, "I wish...I wish...."

"Shh." She pressed a finger to his lips. His entire body felt tense; she began to rub his shoulders and back in an attempt to loosen him up. "Please don't say anything. Life here is so...basic. So simple." Her voice dropped to a whisper. "It's like lying bare on the beach. Unadorned and lovely."

"But there's still New York—"

"Next week," she vowed more strongly. "Not now."

"Then where's the honesty you claim you need?"

"What's honest in New York, New York can have. I just want to enjoy what's here. Now." Her eyes grew beseeching. "Can you understand that, Oliver?"

"Oh, sweetheart, only too well," he murmured with a sudden fierceness. Then his lips sought hers, transmitting that fierceness through her body in the name of passion. His kiss was long and possessive, enduring even as he swept her off her feet and headed for the bedroom. Only when the large bed took her weight did he raise his head. Trembling as he leaned over her, he sighed her name several times and with reverence. "Leslie, Leslie, let me love you the way you should be loved. . . ."

Stunned by the aching depth of his plea, Leslie could find no words to express what she felt. Oliver Ames had to be the most gentle, most compassionate man in the world. Opening her arms, she reached up to him. For just a minute he held her, embracing her with the same fierceness with which he'd kissed her, then gently pressing her away. With unsteady fingers he untied her robe and, spreading it to either side, proceeded to worship every bare inch of her body with his hands, then his mouth, then his tongue. Helplessly she writhed at the havoc he caused, loving every minute of it, loving him all the more. For there was something supremely tender about his lovemaking this time, something that went far beyond the gentleness he'd shown before. It was as though in this abandoned adulation he sought to apologize for what another man had done, to make amends, to tell her what an exquisitely feminine wonder she was.

And she believed. She believed. How could she not, with the warmth of strong, manly fingers stroking her hips, with the wetness of a long, sensual tongue adoring her breast, with the length of lean, sinewed flesh branding her cherished? If she'd thought to protest that it wasn't Oliver's apology to give, her need for his loving was far too great to deny him his penance. His entire goal seemed to be giving her pleasure; yet she reveled in the sound of his own moans and sighs, in the quaking of his limbs when he finally drew back to remove his robe.

Then, wanting to absolve him of guilt for all time, she opened her thighs and welcomed him. The ensuing fire was purgative, cleansing, propelling them onward to a climactic point where it seemed their souls would fuse forever. When, after wave upon wave of glory washed over their straining bodies, they finally cooled, exhaustion took its inevitable toll. Deliriously happy and at peace, Leslie fell asleep in her lover's arms, awakening only when morning had fully established itself over the island.

"Happy Birthday, sweetheart."

She snuggled closer, eyes closed, a smile on her face. "Mmm. You remembered."

The arms around her tightened. The voice by her ear was a deep, lazy hum. "Of course, I remembered. Thirty years old...oops, what's this?"

She felt the hair being lifted from her neck. "What's what?"

"This line."

"What line?"

One long finger sizzled around her throat. "This. Must be your age. They say the neck is the first to show it, love."

Leslie tipped her head back, arched a brow and opened the violet-hued eye beneath it. "Is that so?" she asked smartly.

Oliver nodded, trying his best to keep a straight face. "Uh huh. I should know. In my business, the face is everything. We worry about important things like lines around the mouth and receding hairlines and sagging chins."

"Do you now?" she teased. "And what'll you do when your day is done?"

"Oh, I've got no cause for concern," he stated outrageously. "Men don't get older; they just get more dignified-looking. It's women who have to worry. Say, Les, I wouldn't scowl like that. It'll only bring out lines on your forehead." He ducked in time to avoid the play-

ful swat she aimed at his head, then grabbed her and
kissed her soundly. She protested for only an instant
before surrendering to his morning pleasure. When he
came up for air, his eyes were dark and earnest. "Somehow," he said softly, stroking the delicate lines of her
face, "I don't think you have to worry about wrinkles.
You sure as hell don't look thirty. I may not have
known you five or ten years ago, but I'd guess that
you're one of those women who's getting better, not
older."

"Oliver Ames," Leslie scolded gently, "this sounds
like a living advertisement. Next thing I know the
cameramen will pop out from behind the drapes."

"There aren't any drapes."

"Then. . .from under the bed."

"Heaven help anyone who was under this bed last
night. Poor fool would have a concussion."

She shook her head and sighed through a grin. "You
are incorrigible."

"Better incorrigible than late for breakfast. Come
on," he announced, dropping her onto the sheet as he
rolled out of bed, "I'm hungry." Then he looked down
at her. "On second thought, you stay put. For the birthday girl, breakfast in bed."

The birthday girl, however, was suddenly and acute-
ly aware that she'd never seen Oliver nude in the day-
light. Beneath the bright sun streaking through the
skylights, his body looked very strong and very male.

"Les?" He leaned over her. Startled, she raised her
eyes. "You do want breakfast, don't you?" he whispered.

She swallowed once and realized how silly he'd think
her if she said she just wanted to look at him, to touch
him. "Sure."

As though reading her thoughts, he sat back down on
the sheets. Taking her hand in his, he pressed it to his

hip, moving it gently over the very strip of flesh that all the world had seen. "Maybe I'm feeling my age, after all," he teased. "You gave me quite a workout last night." Leaning forward, he kissed her forehead. "We'll have breakfast and then go . . . exploring. How does that sound?"

The deep velvet of his voice sent shivers of excitement through her, as did the smoothness of his flank. She grinned. "I'd like that." Slipping beneath the sheet, she watched him leave the room and closed her eyes, awaiting his return.

Return he did, bearing a tray filled with all sorts of breakfast goodies. They ate to their hearts' content, then explored as he'd promised. It was nearly noon before they finally climbed from bed, showered together, then headed for the beach wearing nothing but oversize towels, which they proceeded to spread on the sand and lie upon.

"This is indecent," she remarked, eyeing the solid length of Oliver's naked body stretched beside her, "but I love it."

He opened one eye. "You're very daring for a conservative lady. Topless on the public beach, nude here. Say, you never did finish the story of the flower child." He closed his eye and flipped onto his stomach, propping his chin on his hands in time to see her bob up.

"Wait," she said, "if you're going to switch on me, you need more lotion." She had the bottle in her hand and was kneeling at his hips, grateful for the excuse to touch him. He shivered when she drizzled a line of cream down his spine. "Wouldn't want your butt to get burned."

"God forbid," he muttered, burying his face in his arms to endure the agony of the hands working so diligently over his skin. It was a full minute after she'd finished and lain down again before he thought to look up. Shifting in a vain attempt to make himself comfortable, he cleared his throat. "Your story."

She was on her back, arms and legs restful, eyes closed, face to the sun. As an afterthought, she rubbed the lotion lingering on her hands over her stomach and breasts, then fell still. "Not much more to tell."

"Did you transfer back east to finish school?"

"And jeopardize my independence? No way."

"It didn't bother you to be out there with memories of that fellow all around?"

"I was so angry at the time that I was thinking only of the discomfort he'd feel knowing I was there. When the anger faded, I realized that there wasn't an awful lot left. Yes, I was hurt and embarrassed and more than a little disillusioned. But I knew that it'd be worse to fly back home with my tail between my legs. Besides, I liked Berkeley and what with the course load I took on, I had plenty to keep me busy. I graduated a semester early and taught for six months before going back to grad school. By that time I'd accepted what had happened with Joe."

"So you came home."

She nodded. "I'd done a lot of growing up during those three and a half years. Not only was I the wiser for my experience with Joe, but I realized that I was a strong enough person to hold my own among the Parishes. And, as it happens, I love New York."

Eyes closed, he groped for her hand, finding it, enveloping it in his. "Look who sounds like an ad, now? And I thought you didn't like crowds."

"I don't...when it comes to going to work or the bank or the dry cleaner or the supermarket. But I love museums and the theater, and there's nothing more delightful than bundling up and strolling down a packed Fifth Avenue at Christmastime. That's why I live outside the city but within easy reach. If I don't feel like

reaching, I don't. I have the choice." Oliver's respectful
chuckle brought her head around. "What about you?
Doesn't it bother you—living right in the thick of
things?" He'd previously told her that he lived in the
city, though he hadn't elaborated either on where or on
what kind of place he had.

He shrugged. "For the convenience of it, I'd put up
with most anything. Besides, I have a small place in the
Berkshires. Great for weekends."

She wondered what he did on those weekends,
whether he had someone to play Scrabble with and...
do other things with. But she didn't ask. She didn't feel
she had the right. After all, there had been no lofty words
of love or proclamations of undying devotion. She didn't
want them. They could be so very shallow. *No,* she
mused, *better to assume nothing than to pin false hopes
on something that would probably never materialize.* It
was far safer this way. Safer, if discouraging....

"You're awfully quiet," Oliver whispered.

She tossed off his concern with a shrug. "Just...
thinking."

"About what?"

"About...how beautiful it is down here and how
much I wish I could stay another week." Though round-
about, it was the truth.

He was up on an elbow. "Can't you?"

Feeling his gaze, she shook her head and smiled, but
didn't open her eyes. "The centers await." She gave an
exaggerated sigh. "Ah me, the price of success. For us
lady executives, the day is never done. They depend on
us," she drawled. "They need us. Oh, to be a lowly er-
rand girl—hey, what are you doing?" She opened her
eyes with a start to find Oliver on his haunches by her
hip.

"Lotioning you up." His hands were already at work
spreading the cream he'd gushed on.

"But I'm already lotioned!" Feeling her body's instant reaction to his touch, she twisted to the side. Oliver simply straddled her hips to hold her still. "Oliver . . ." she warned, lying flat, looking up at him. His hands slid over her skin in a pattern of sensuous circles, teasing by sheer impartiality. "Oliver!" she whispered more urgently. "This is ridiculous! The oldest trick in the book—seduction by suntan lotion!"

"Guess I'm not terribly original then," he murmured, slithering his hands over the peak of her breasts again and again.

"My God!" she moaned. She bit her lip and arched helplessly into his touch.

"No, sweetheart, just me." Planting his hands on either side of her shoulders, he stretched his full length over her. His eyes held the lambency she'd come to know, the depth she'd come to love, the vulnerability that could touch her every time. "Just me . . . needing you again."

Leslie coiled her arms around his neck. "I don't know about these male model types. They're insatiable."

"Only with you," he murmured, seeking the honey of her mouth as he nudged a place for himself between her thighs.

And she believed . . . again. She believed because she had to, because the intense love that swelled within her came part and parcel with trust. If she was wrong, she'd be later damned. But for now she had no choice. No choice at all.

"This is positively decadent," Leslie remarked. "I don't think we've been properly dressed for two days."

It was Saturday morning, and they'd just emerged from an early-morning swim. She blotted her towel over her face, then glanced up to find Oliver just standing there, dripping wet, looking down at her. His towel hung, forgotten, in his hand, but she, too, forgot it in the face of his strangely uncertain expression. She'd seen that expression more than once in the past two days. It was not quite haunted, not quite pained, not quite worried, not quite fearful, yet it held a bit of all of those emotions and more, thrown together to produce something that cut to her heart, then twisted and turned.

"Are you all right?" she asked softly. She took a step forward, then was stopped by a sudden sense of foreboding. Shaking her head, she moved forward again. "Oliver?"

He blinked and inhaled. "Sorry, Les. I missed that."

Very gently, using her own towel, she began to dry his chest. "Didn't miss much. I was only being smart."

"Again?" His cockeyed smile was a relief, as was the mischievous eye that warmed her length. "You know, we really should get dressed," he suggested, tugging her against him. "It's been nearly two days. Think we'll remember how?"

At first she thought he was mocking her. After all, hadn't she just commented on their seemingly perpetual state of undress? But he looked so innocent and sounded so sincere. Where had his mind been then? She'd noticed his tension of late, a tension coming at odd moments such as the one just past. What was he thinking?

It was getting more difficult. Each day of bliss made it worse. *Think of today, only today*, Leslie told herself. But it didn't work. There was tomorrow, and the tomorrow after that...and so on until she was back in New York. Would she see Oliver then? Could she possibly reconcile her far slower life-style with his faster one? Did she want to? Did he want her to? All she knew was that she wanted Oliver. Very desperately.

"Hey, what's this?" he asked with exquisite tenderness as he dabbed a tear from the corner of her eye. Without awaiting her answer, he closed his arms about her and hugged her tightly.

"I don't think I like the idea of getting dressed," she said in a soft, sad voice.

"Neither do I, but we'll have to sooner or later. You know that, don't you, Les?" His deeper meaning was as glaring as the sun upon open waters.

"Oh, yes."

He drew his head back to look at her. His jaw was tight, his expression closed. "You also know that I'm not letting you go, don't you?"

His vehemence surprised her as much as it pleased her. "No, I didn't know that," she whispered.

"Do you mind?"

She shook her head. Mind? *Mind?* The first hint that he wanted to see her back in New York...how could she possibly mind? True, there'd be mammoth hurdles to clear. True, she might stumble and fall. But...what if she took it one day at a time, much as she'd tried to do here? Wouldn't it be better than nothing at all?

"Of course I don't mind," she answered, eyes misty, a smile on her lips.

"Good. Then what say we get dressed and go into town. There's something I want to pick up."

"Sounds fine."

"And brunch on the quai, a drive around the island, the afternoon on the beach?"

"Um hmm."

"And dinner...a last night out?"

She swallowed down the knot that was so very quick to form. "You bet."

He kissed her then, each eye in turn, then the tip of her nose, then her mouth. Sucking in a shaky breath, he hugged her tight, then, head down, moved back and took her hand. Leslie could have sworn he was as affected by the moment as she, but how much of what she saw was a product of what she wanted to see, she didn't know. Wishful thinking was a dangerous thing. Dangerous...though irresistible.

IT WAS A BUSY DAY, this, their last full one on St. Barts. By unspoken design, they kept their minds occupied with the pleasure of what they saw, said and did. It was as though each feared the thoughts that, given idleness, might creep in and begin to fester.

Gustavia seemed more alive than ever. They walked, then brunched—then, to Leslie's horror, stopped at the jewelry shop Oliver had obviously visited earlier that week, to pick up a beautiful gold necklace he'd purchased. It was a serpentine chain whose central links had been removed to make way for a single amethyst. The stone matched her eyes perfectly. Only when he lifted the chain from its box and started to put it around her neck, though, did she realize he'd bought it for her.

"I can't accept this, Oliver," she breathed. "It's...it's too much!"

"Not too much. Just right. It was made for you, your birthday present. I'm sorry it's late." He deftly hooked the clasp, then straightened the chain and stood back to admire the way it nestled against her skin.

Leslie raised a trembling finger to touch the warm amethyst. "But you didn't have to— There was no need...." Then, embarrassed, she scowled. "Tony didn't put you up to this, did he?"

For a minute she thought Oliver would hit her. His eyes grew dark, his features fierce. "No, Tony didn't put me up to it. I thought of it all by myself."

"I'm sorry," she said quickly, reaching out to grasp his arm, "that wasn't what I meant." In pain, she looked down. "It's just that it's so beautiful...and the thought that went into it.... I...I wanted, needed to know the thought was yours." Dropping her hand, she turned away. "I guess I'm not very good at accepting gifts. So often they've either been too easily come by, or given with an ulterior motive."

"Oh, sweetheart," he moaned and turned her to him. Placing his hands on her shoulders, he lowered his head to look at her. Her eyes lifted slowly as he spoke. "I want you to have this just . . . because."

"Just . . . because?" she echoed timidly.

"Just because you're you and I'm me, and together we've had a pretty wonderful week. I want you to have this so that when we get back to New York—" his features stiffened imperceptibly "—you'll be able to touch your throat and remember what we've shared."

"I could never forget," she murmured, entranced by the goodness he exuded. "Never, Oliver."

"I hope not," he rasped, then crushed her against him with a kind of desperation that was to remain with them through the rest of their stay. It poked its head through the palm fronds when they played on the beach that afternoon. It was propped between the salt and pepper shakers when they had dinner out that evening.

Later that night their lovemaking was slower and more intense than it had been. It was an expression of all the things they'd meant to each other during the week— of fresh lemonade, wine and cheese and Scrabble, of gentle and intimate talk about nothing in particular, of loving and living and counting one's blessings for the moment, of a gold chain with an amethyst at its heart. Particularly when they awoke again at dawn to desire and to each other was there a desperation in it, a kind of grasping and seeking and holding to something that might never come again. For that was precisely what Leslie feared. With the north would come the cold and the real world and all the differences she could only imagine to exist between herself and this man who'd made such a thorough conquest of her heart.

As a couple boarding the small island-hopper Sunday at noon, they were subdued. Transferring to the larger jet on St. Martin, they were distracted. Arriving in New York in the dark to subfreezing temperatures, they were visibly tense. Only when Oliver put Leslie in a cab headed for her home on the island, though, did she come close to breaking.

"Oliver?" She raised a frantic gaze to his, prepared to blurt out her love, prepared to plead, prepared to do most anything to prolong the inevitable parting.

"Shh. I'll call you. Okay?"

Don't call me. I'll call you. Her heart plummeted to her frigid toes. "Okay." She flashed him a plastic smile, swallowed hard, then turned and let the driver take her home.

7

OLIVER STOOD AT THE CURB for what seemed hours after Leslie's cab had pulled away. With his eyes he followed it as it dodged other vehicles and slowed, then entered the airport's exit road and sped forward, finally disappearing around the bend that would take it to the parkway and on to her home.

A part of him was in the cab. He wasn't sure how or when it had happened—whether he'd first fallen in love with her honest smile or her ready wit or her breasts in the sun or her mushroom omelets. Hell, it might have been the lavender leprechaun, stuffed-up and sneezing, for whom he'd first fallen. But he'd fallen. No doubt about that. He'd fallen hard. And, damn it, he didn't know what to do!

He'd made a mess of it with his whimsy of shaking the image and existing solely as a man. It had backfired! He'd simply been pigeonholed differently.

Leslie knew him as a model. Oh, yes, it had had its moments, and it was certainly flattering. Only trouble was that she loved him. He was sure of it. Leslie, who believed in, who needed honesty above all, was in love with a man who had deceived her from the start.

"Hey, fella, we're holdin' up the line. You wanna cab or not?"

Snapped from his brooding, Oliver looked down at the body sprawled from the driver's seat toward the passenger's window, at the face scowling up at him. With a curt nod he opened the back door, picked up his bags and tossed them in, then followed them. After giving his Manhattan address to the cabbie, he slouched against the door, his fist pressed to his mouth, and stared blindly into the arena of headlights and taillights they entered.

Was it deceit? Or simply evasion? He'd never lied, but had told only half the truth. He did model, though it was purely a hobby and something he did far less frequently than he'd let Leslie believe. If only he *could* model more often! But his practice was more demanding than it had ever been. Demanding, challenging...rewarding. Even now he wondered what bizarre messages he'd find awaiting him when he got home. Then his thoughts turned to Leslie, and he lost interest in bizarre messages.

She'd been as upset as he when they'd left St. Barts. A healthy tan notwithstanding, she'd looked as pale as her hand had felt cold. They'd said little to each other. He knew she'd hoped for something, but he'd been stymied.

He'd tried. He had tried. Even if she hated him when she learned the truth, she'd have to admit that he'd tried. And every time, she'd hushed him, saying she hadn't wanted to know, that it wasn't important. So why hadn't he pushed? He'd always been strong and convincing, never one to let a woman deter him when he'd had something to do or say. But...he'd never been in love before. And Leslie was a woman like no other he'd known.

The cab swerved. The cabbie swore. From his slouched position Oliver muttered an oath and thrust a hand through his hair. New York looked ugly, all dark and gray and spattered with mud from the snow that must have recently fallen. So different from the sunshine and heat of St. Barts. Damn, but he felt cold inside!

Seeking warmth, he wearily dropped his head back

and conjured up memories from the week now past. It worked for a time. As the cab sped onward, snaking in and out of the parkway traffic, he thought of the villa, the beach, bubbling Gustavia . . . and Leslie through it all. The times he'd spent alone at the start of the week had mysteriously fallen from mind. The images that remained were of time they'd spent together—living, laughing, loving.

But Oliver Ames, more than most, knew that one couldn't exist wholly in a world of memories. In addition to past, one needed present and future. Present and future. The present was a dingy cab fighting its way across town now, through congested Manhattan streets. The future was a confrontation he feared as he'd never feared anything before. So much was at stake. So very much.

The cab lurched through the Sunday-evening traffic, forging steadily onward until at last it came to an abrupt halt at the door of his building. Oliver dug his wallet from his trousers' pocket, thinking how strange it felt in his hand after a week without it. He tugged out several bills and paid the cabbie, then hauled himself and his belongings from the cab.

The doorman was on the spot. "Good evening, Dr. Ames. Would you like a hand?"

Oliver dipped his head in response to the greeting, held up a hand in refusal of the offer, then headed through the door that the attendant had opened. Eighteen floors later, he was in his own apartment.

Leaving his bags by the door, he easily found his way in the darkness down the two steps into the sunken living room, where he collapsed in a sofa and dropped his head into his hands. Then, propping his chin on his palms, he studied the dark.

He missed her already. It was so quiet here. Not that she made much noise, but just knowing she might be in another room would have lightened the atmosphere of the place.

What was he going to do? For three days now, since Thursday, when they'd spent the day together and then made love and he'd realized just how deeply he was in over his head, he'd been trying to decide. He could call her right now and blurt out the truth, counting on her love to master her anger. Or he could make a date for tomorrow night or Tuesday night, and then tell her the truth. He could send her a letter of confession and follow it up with two dozen long-stemmed roses. Or he could storm over to her place and confess it all in person. As a last resort, he could always abduct her, break the news, then hold her prisoner until she forgave him.

Damn Joe Durand! It sounded as though Leslie had been leery enough of deception before Joe had come along, but his shoddy treatment of her had cemented her feelings. Now Oliver had inadvertently stepped in the muck Joe had left, and his feet were stuck. He felt like such a heel! A heel!

Eyes wide, he threw his head back, then gave a savage push and left the sofa. Flipping on the lights by the door, he grabbed his bags, strode angrily down the hall to his bedroom, tossed the cases onto the bed, then stood glaring at them.

"Damn!" Crossing to the bedstand phone, he picked up the receiver, held it midair for a minute, then scowled at it and slammed it down. He stormed back down the hall, paused overlooking the living room and stood, hands on his hips, frowning.

He lived in the lap of luxury in this coop with its prestigious East Side address. Maybe she wouldn't be surprised at it; after all, she'd assumed him to be a successful model, and they reportedly did well. Rubbing a tired hand against the taut muscles at the back of his neck, he slowly descended the steps and perched on the arm of a chair.

He liked this place. He'd certainly worked hard enough for it. Plush carpeting, cushiony upholstered sofas and chairs, lacquered coffee tables and wall units bearing unique mementos from one trip or another—a far cry from the cramped duplex his parents had rented all those years. He thought of the pleasant garden condominium he'd recently helped them buy, and smiled. They were comfortable; they deserved it.

In its idle wandering, his gaze tripped over loose pillows of the same rich browns and beiges and grays as the rest of the room before falling on the ancient brass spittoon he'd picked up in Wales. It was a planter now, bearing a small fig tree. Standing, he walked over to finger the oval leaves. It wasn't doing well—it needed sun and warmth. He snorted. *He* needed sun and warmth, but his sun and warmth was Leslie. Did he look as despairing as the poor fig tree in front of him?

The jangle of the phone startled him. His head flew toward the kitchen. It was his private line ringing, not the business phone he kept in the den. In two strides he'd covered the distance and snatched up the phone.

"Hello?"

"Oliver, you're back! It's Tony. How did it go?"

"How're ya doin', Tony?" Oliver asked, trying to cover up his disappointment. For a split second he'd hoped it would be Leslie.

"Not bad...but tell me about *you*." His voice grew cautious. "She wasn't angry, was she?"

"As a matter of fact," Oliver began with a sigh, "she wasn't thrilled at first. But she came around."

Tony grinned. "I knew she would. You've got charm, friend. I knew you could handle her. It was a good week, then?"

"Great. You were right. The villa's gorgeous. So's the island. Bright sun every day. It never rained."

"Come on, Oliver. This is the guy you sweat with on the tennis court twice a month. I don't want a camp letter. I want some of that gut-spilling you guys love to provoke. Was it a good week?"

"It was a great week."

"And?"

"Any more is private."

"She's my sister, Ames. I wouldn't have sent you down there if I hadn't had hopes that you two might hit if off."

"Hit if off...." Oliver smirked, rather amused by his friend's impatience. "You mean...*make* it?"

"I mean like each other." Tony grimaced. "The woman's impossible. I've tried again and again to introduce her to men I think she'll like, but she's just not interested. My happening to know the man in the Homme Premier ad was a bolt out of the blue."

Oliver shot a glance at the ceiling. "So it was a fix-up after all. Strange, I thought it was supposed to be a joke," he remarked grimly. Of course he'd known better than that. Tony Parish was transparent, at least when he, too, was sweating it out on the courts. But it didn't bother him to string Tony along. He needed someone to blame for the mess he was in.

"You didn't hurt her," Tony came back more quietly.

"No. I didn't hurt her. At least not yet."

Once more, deadly calm. "What are you talking about?"

Oliver rested one hand low on his hip and hung his head. "We had a wonderful week together. It was... unbelievable."

"So?"

"So—" he took a breath "—I think your sister's fallen in love with a man she believes to be a very glamorous male model."

"Male model? Didn't you tell her the truth?"

"That is the truth . . . albeit only a tiny part."

"And you didn't tell her the rest?" came the disbelieving voice.

"No."

Tony swore softly, then began to pace within the limits of the telephone cord. "You picked a great one to lie to—"

"I didn't lie."

"Then you picked a great one to be evasive with. Jeez, I don't believe it. I was sure you'd tell her everything within the first day or two. You're almost as straitlaced as she is!" He paced another round. "Do you have any idea what my sister thinks of deception? She's pretty opinionated on that score. Do you?"

"I didn't, then. I do now."

Tony had paused in his ranting long enough to hear the dejection in Oliver's voice. "Are you all right?" he asked, cautious again.

"No, I'm not!" Oliver exploded, his own frustration needing outlet. "I've got to figure out some way of telling Leslie what I do without having her positively despise me for not having told her in the first place. I'm *not* all right. It's become an emotional issue; she's apt to hate me."

The voice on the other end of the line was instantly contrite. "And that matters to you?"

"Damned right it matters! Not that I'd particularly want you for a brother-in-law knowing that you concocted this cock-and-bull scheme in the first place . . . !"

Satisfied, Tony sat down in his chair. "She was the one with the idea, Oliver," he said indulgently. "I simply set it into motion."

"Same difference. Damn, it's hard."

"Can I help?"

"Don't you dare. As a matter of fact, don't you dare

repeat a word of this conversation to Leslie! I may have
made a mess of things, but it's my mess, and I'll be the
one to clean it up."

"She's got fire in her."

He gave a wry nod. "Tell me."

"Think you can handle her?"

"I'll handle her."

"Okay, pal." Tony was smiling broadly. "And
Oliver?"

"Yeah?"

The smile grew more mischievous. "Good luck." If
anyone could handle Leslie Parish, her brother mused,
Oliver Ames could. Despite this minor and surely temporary misunderstanding, things had worked out well
indeed.

Oliver wasn't in quite as optimistic a frame of mind
when he hung up the phone. Love did strange things to
otherwise rational people. It made them lose perspective
and overreact. That was what he wanted to avoid.

Back in the living room, he opened the bar and
poured himself a drink. Its warmth was the first he'd felt
since...since he'd made love to Leslie so early that
morning. Just that morning—it was hard to believe. He
remembered every sweet moment; even now could feel
the fragile shape of her in his hands. She'd been so
honest and giving in her lovemaking. She'd lived true to
her word. Not for a minute, though she hadn't said it
aloud, had she hidden from him the fact of her love.
And not for a minute did Oliver believe that he was
vainly imagining it. He hadn't asked for love, hadn't
gone looking for it. But feeling the all-consuming need
he had to be with and share with and do for Leslie, seeing an identical desire written on her face time and
again, he knew. Leslie loved him. He loved her. All that
remained was for him to tell her what he'd done and
why.

Bidden in part by determination, in part by the sheer need to hear her voice, he returned to the kitchen and lifted the phone. Information quickly gave him her number. As quickly he punched it out. The phone rang once, then a second time.

"Hello?" She sounded breathless, as though she'd come running.

"Leslie?"

A smile lit her voice. "Hi," she said softly.

"You got home all right," he ventured likewise.

"Uh huh. And you?"

"Fine." The sound of her voice was an instant balm. Perched atop his high kitchen stool, he felt himself begin to relax. "How are you?"

"Okay. I'm . . . cold."

"I know the feeling." It was only incidentally related to the abrupt change in temperature to which their bodies had been exposed in the past few hours. "Your house was okay? No problems?" She lived in a small Tudor home on a wooded lot, she'd said. He worried about her being so alone.

"Just quiet." Her voice fell to a whisper. "And lonely."

"I miss you," he murmured in lieu of taking her in his arms and kissing her loneliness away.

"Me too." She paused then and, sensing that she wanted to go on, he gave her time. "Oliver," she began again and timidly, "when will I see you?"

The utter smallness of her voice cut him to the quick. He could imagine how she'd fought asking. She'd want to be sophisticated and cool and unclinging. He hated himself for having forced her hand, though he found solace in this further evidence of her love.

"That's why I'm calling, sweetheart. I'd like us to spend next weekend together. Just the two of us at my place up north. I could pick you up Friday night and have you back Sunday. How about it?"

"I'd love to, Oliver." Her voice glowed. In turn he smiled.

"I wish it could be sooner. Friday sounds so far off. But this week will be crammed . . . after last."

Her laugh was a light, airy sound that made him float. "What is it this week . . . say, what *do* you do, other than cologne?"

His bubble threatened to burst. "Oh, clothing and stuff. Have you spoken to Tony?"

"Not yet. I'll have to give him a call to thank him for my . . . birthday present." Her voice lowered. "Thank you again."

"For what?"

"For . . . taking care of me when I was sick, for making the rest of the week so wonderful, for the necklace."

"Are you wearing it now?" Closing his eyes he pictured her as she'd stood before him last night, wearing nothing but the moonlight and that strip of gold with its amethyst eye.

"Yes. I'm wearing it," she murmured shyly.

"I'm glad." He smiled, then realized that he could sit forever saying small nothings to her. But he wanted to tell her he loved her—and he feared doing that. "Well, then, how does six on Friday sound? We can stop for dinner on the way."

"Sounds perfect."

"I'll be looking forward to it." His voice was suddenly lower and faintly hoarse.

"Me too."

"Take care, Les."

"You too. And Oliver?"

"Yes?"

"I . . . I . . . thanks for calling."

"Sure thing, sweetheart. See you Friday."

For several minutes after hanging up the phone, he sat where he was, basking in the glow that lingered. She was a wonder . . . so thoroughly lovable. And she'd had more courage than he. She'd nearly said it. *I love you.* Why couldn't he say the words? He admitted them freely to himself, had even implied them to Tony. Was it that he'd feel hypocritical telling Leslie he loved her while he knew he'd been less than forthright on other matters? Was it that he feared she might not believe him in *this* when he finally did confess to his deception?

The glow was gone by the time he stood up, replaced by a shroud of concern. He'd tell her this weekend after they arrived at his place. They'd be isolated and, aside from his own car, more or less stranded. She'd be stuck with him. She'd have to hear him out. And he'd have the whole weekend to prove his love one way or the other.

That decided, he returned to the front hall and picked up the thick pile of waiting mail. An hour later he retreated to the den, pushed several buttons on his telephone console and sprawled out on the dark leather sofa with an arm over his eyes to listen to the phone messages for the week.

An hour after that he was ready to return to St. Barts.

LESLIE, TOO, had gone through her mail and then taken to the phone, but in a more active capacity.

"Tony?"

"Les! How are you?"

"Great." Silence. She was grinning like a Cheshire cat. "Thanks, Tony. It was a super birthday present."

"Liked it?" he asked smugly.

"Uh huh."

"I thought you would. He's quite a guy."

"Uh huh."

"So." It was like pulling teeth, in addition to which, he felt decidedly duplicitous. "Will you be seeing him again?"

"Uh huh." Her pulse sped at the thought. "He's got a place in the Berkshires. We're going up this weekend."

"Great!" he exclaimed. So Oliver had decided to make his pitch in the Berkshires. Secluded. Romantic. *Good luck, pal.*

"How's everything here, Tony?"

"Fine. Busy. Dad's still in Phoenix."

"Still? I thought he was due back last week."

"He was. . . ."

She smiled. "But the golfing was too good."

Tony chuckled. "Something like that."

"And the kids are well?"

"Raising Cain in the other room. You mean you can't hear the noise?"

"Why aren't they in bed?"

"Because it's back to school tomorrow. And the law of adolescence says that one positively cannot be awake and aware on the morning following a school vacation. Heaven forbid they should be in condition to learn."

She laughed. "Perverse little things, aren't they? So why isn't their father laying down a law of his own?"

"Because he's talking with you."

"Oh. Good reason. Well, then I won't keep you long. I want to give Bren and Diane calls anyway. They're both doin' all right?"

"Brenda's fine. The kids had a ball skiing. She and Larry have about had it with lugging skis and poles and boots back and forth to the slopes, but otherwise Vail was to their liking." He paused, frowning. "Diane's the one who's got me worried."

"What's wrong?"

"I'm not sure. She's been behaving really strangely. She took off by herself last Monday and Tuesday, had Brad worried to death until he finally found a note buried at the bottom of the mail."

Leslie, too, was worried. Diane had always been a little high-strung, and it was obvious that she hadn't been happy of late, but she'd never disappeared before. "Where was she?"

"In a hotel."

"In the city?"

"Uh huh. Just sitting by herself. Thinking, she said. I couldn't get much more out of her. When she came home Tuesday night she was pretty subdued."

"How have things been going for her at the office?"

Tony sighed. "According to Gaffney, things have been tough. She's difficult to work with and getting worse all the time. Demanding and unpredictable. Very temperamental. Why don't you give her a call, Les? Maybe you can find out what's bothering her."

Leslie gave a facetious grunt. "I know what's bothering her. It's Brad."

"Come on. Brad's not that bad."

"Tony, he's fooling around, and you know it!"

"What else is new?"

"Diane knows it, too. Discretion has never been one of his stronger points."

"Yeah, but a lot of the time it's just talk—"

"Which can be nearly as hurtful."

"Come on, Les. I can't believe that Diane would be threatened by talk. Brad wouldn't go out of his way to humiliate her."

"You're sure of that?" she asked skeptically.

Tony hesitated, then gave vent to his own frustration. "Of course I'm not sure! The guy may be a great businessman, but we've never been terribly close. I can't know what he'd do. All I do know is that if Di doesn't shape up, he may have just cause to wander."

"That's an awful thing to say, Tony, particularly since he's the thing preventing her from shaping up! Okay, I'll grant that Diane's had other problems. But can you imagine how she must feel when she hears about each of Brad's little . . . diversions? *Your* wife was a wanderer. How did you feel?"

"A low blow, Les."

"And well aimed. How did you feel?"

He pondered her question, then spoke with uncharacteristic seriousness. Gone was all pretense of the invincible male. Left was a man whose home life had fallen apart. "Angry. Hurt. Confused. Embarrassed. Insecure."

Much the same way Leslie had felt when she'd discovered that Joe Durand was married. Much the way she couldn't help but feel at the thought of Oliver with . . . other women. . . .

"Thank you for being so honest," she said more gently. "Now try to think of Diane living with, or trying to live with, those same feelings."

There was a meaningful silence. "Isn't that something she's got to work out with Brad? We can't give her much more than emotional support."

"Exactly. Let me call her. Maybe she'll talk to me. Sometimes just being able to air things helps."

"You know, Les," Tony breathed over the phone, "you're a good person."

"I'm her sister."

"There was a time way back then when you wanted nothing to do with the Parishes," he reminded her softly. "We thought we'd lost you to the West Coast."

"I needed breathing room, Tony. I still do. I guess I'm just fortunate in that I've found plenty of it."

She heard a riot of sounds in the background, then Tony's voice aimed away from the phone. "Leave him alone, Jason! If you boys don't . . . . Mark, go upstairs!" The voice returned. "Listen, hon, I've got to run."

"So I hear. Go ahead, Tony. I'll call Di. And . . . thanks again for Oliver."

Her brother smiled warmly. "My pleasure. And many happy returns."

Mirroring his smile, Leslie hung up the phone. Memories of Oliver warmed her for the moment. Then, unable to shake her concern, Leslie did put in a call to Diane. A disgruntled Brad announced that she was in her room reading and had left orders not to be disturbed. Reluctant to force the issue and possibly increase the tension between husband and wife, Leslie simply left word that she'd call the next day.

It was easier said than done. Round and about her own hectic schedule, she tried to reach Diane at the office three times. Each time she was out. It was not until after dinner that evening that Leslie finally made contact. What ensued was the most unproductive conversation she'd ever held with another adult human being.

"Di?" When there was no sound of recognition, she identified herself. "It's me. Leslie." When there was still no sound, she prodded gently. "Are you there?"

"Yes."

"How are you?" When again there was silence, she babbled on. "I tried you last night after I got back from St. Barts, but you were reading."

"I'm okay."

"Are you sure? You sound awful."

"Thanks."

"I didn't mean that in offense. Just concern." Silence. "Is everything all right there?"

"Yes."

She dared. "Brad's okay?"

"Yes."

"Hey, I'm not interrupting dinner, am I?" There had to be some excuse for her sister's curtness. Perhaps she and Brad were in the middle of a fight, and Brad was standing right there.

"No."

"Listen, maybe we could meet for lunch one day this week."

"Maybe. I'll get back to you."

"How about Wednesday?" Leslie blurted. Tomorrow sounded too obvious.

"I don't know. I'll have to get back to you."

"Will you?" Even in the best of times, Diane was notoriously bad at returning calls. It was one of the things her business associates were always yelling about.

"Yes."

"Try to make it Wednesday."

"I'll call you."

"Please, Di. I'd really like to talk." Leslie tried to make it sound as though she were the one with the problem. The subtle suggestion went right over her sister's head.

"I said I'd call you," Diane snapped back impatiently.

"Okay, Di. Talk with you then."

Diane hung up the phone without another word, at which point Leslie promptly called Brenda. Between them they were no closer to knowing what to do about Diane.

"Maybe something happened at the office?" Leslie suggested in trying to explain Diane's sudden turn for the worse.

Brenda sighed. "Possible. Not probable."

As Leslie had talked with Tony, she now raised the issue of their sister's shaky emotional state with Brenda. "So what do we do?" she asked. Of the three other Parishes, Brenda was the only one she'd ever leaned on. Capable and serious in business matters, Brenda had a level head on her shoulders. Ironically, the errors she'd made in her personal life were attributable to this very compulsion for order.

"We keep the lines of communication open. You'll have lunch with her Wednesday—"

"Wait a minute. I was the one who proposed Wednesday. Diane refused to commit herself. I'd put money on the fact that she won't even call me."

"Then you'll call her again. Try tomorrow night. Bug her until she caves in."

"I'm telling you, Bren, she really did sound like stone."

"I know. But she'll be all right."

"Maybe she needs professional help," Leslie ventured cautiously, though she could have predicted Brenda's response. None of the Parishes were fans of psychiatry, though Brenda was worse than the others. A computer person at heart, she believed there to be a sane, systematic, physical explanation for just about everything that happened in life. When her first marriage fell apart, she considered it a victim of the occupational hazard of being a full-time working mother. There simply had not been hours enough in her life to accommodate a demanding husband. Larry, her second, was a warmer, more easygoing man who was very satisfied to take Brenda when she was free. In turn, Brenda seemed free more often, though she'd never admit to the deep emotional need she had for Larry. He, saint that he was, was confident enough not to demand such a confession.

"A shrink?" Brenda asked with obvious distaste. "I doubt it. No, there has to be something more immediate that's causing her to clam up and act strangely. You're right. She's always been shaky. Which is all the more reason why something's got to have triggered her now."

"Well," Leslie sighed, discouraged, "I'll try to get her out with me. I'll let you know what happens."

As though her mind's computer had filed one document and called up another, Brenda's voice lightened. "Hey, you haven't told me about your trip."

Her trip. Mention of it brought an instant spot of warmth to her heart, an instant glow to her cheeks. "It was great." How much did Brenda know? Had Tony told her about his little "joke"?

"Lots of sun?"

Brenda's what-else-is-new tone said it all. She knew nothing. And Leslie wasn't about to enlighten her until she herself felt more sure of Oliver. On St. Barts he'd been unswervingly attentive. Back here, though, even in spite of a weekend date, it remained to be seen whether his seeming affection would hold up. Once he got back out in that faster, glittery world of his. . . .

"Yup," she answered with feigned lightness. "Lots of sun. I got a great tan."

"And rest?"

"That, too."

"Good. Okay, then, you'll keep me posted on Di?"

"Uh huh. Bye-bye, Bren."

Leslie hung up the phone thinking of Oliver. She'd been thrilled to hear from him earlier, after having spent the first agonizing hour at home convinced that he'd never call. Life on St. Barts had been so simple. Life in New York—ah, that was another matter. Theoretically, if she loved Oliver and he loved her, nothing could be simpler. But she could only guess at Oliver's feelings. He was a model and hence, to a certain extent, an actor. On St. Barts she would have sworn he loved her, but that had been part of the illusion she'd chosen to live. Back here, she just didn't know.

The weekend would only be telling to a point. He'd have had five full days to compare her with his other life. If he called on Thursday offering a lame excuse to cancel the weekend, she'd know. But even if the weekend went on as proposed and he was as wonderful as he'd been on St. Barts, would she be able to know for sure that he wasn't simply reliving his vacation fun, simply lusting his way through the weekend, using his home in the Berkshires as a substitute for the villa on St.

Barts? Would she ever really know his feelings? More important, could she trust him fully enough to believe them? When she was with him, trust was automatic. But at moments away—at times such as these, of which there would be more and more—she doubted.

FOR LESLIE, the week was a trying one, filled with highs and lows and very little in between. While it was wonderful getting back to work, wonderful being at work where her mind could be occupied, her free time was quite the opposite. She thought of the restlessness she'd felt so strongly before she'd ever left for vacation, and she realized—as she had on St. Barts—what ailed her. The house was quiet. Meals alone were not really meals at all. Despite a backlog of paperwork, evenings dragged. And an empty bed—an empty bed was cold and forbidding. Yet her thoughts of Oliver fluctuated violently. At times she was so very hopeful, so very buoyant and in love. At other times she was as down in the dumps as Diane appeared to be.

Ironically Diane's depression was the only thing that, in Leslie's free hours, gave her respite from her own love woes. As predicted, she didn't hear from Diane. Giving her the benefit of the doubt Leslie waited until Wednesday morning to call, striking out at the office, finally reaching her at home. No, she wasn't sick. No, she couldn't make it for lunch. No, she couldn't talk just then. Leslie hung up the phone more convinced than ever that something very definitely was wrong. On Wednesday night, with nothing better to do but brood about Oliver, she got in her car and drove to Diane's.

Brad answered the door. He was a man of average height, average looks, above-average business acumen and superaverage ego. Beyond that, he was thoroughly charming in a thoroughly contrived way.

He smiled broadly. "Leslie! What a surprise. We

weren't expecting you. How are you?" He stood aside to let her in out of the cold but left the door conspicuously open.

"I'm fine. How are you, Brad?"

"Very well. Hey, nice tan you've got there. You must have been somewhere warm."

Diane hadn't told him. Well, Leslie reasoned, there was nothing so awful about that. Diane would have no cause to keep Brad informed of the details of her family's comings and goings. "I spent last week at the villa. It was beautiful. Is Diane in?"

He shot her his most regretful smile. "She's in but she's sleeping."

"Sleeping? It's so early. Is she all right?"

"Fine. She's fine. Just been working hard, and I think it's tiring her. She's been concentrating on some new designs for the fall line."

"I see." It wouldn't pay to say that Diane had been out of the office every time Leslie had called. "You're sure she's not angry with me? I've been trying to talk with her since I got back, and she's been practically incommunicado."

Brad gave a loud laugh. "That's Diane," he said, then feigned a conspiratorial whisper. "It's the prima donna in her. I'm sure she's not angry. She'll get back to you as soon as things clear up a little."

On the surface the words were innocent. Delivered by Brad, however, who stood with his hand on the open door, they bore deeper meaning. Leslie felt distinctly unwelcome.

She shifted her stance and fingered her keys. "Well, then, I won't disturb you. You will call me if there's any problem, won't you?"

"What problem could there possibly be?" Brad asked, throwing his arm around her shoulder in a spurious show of affection that successfully turned her toward the door. *Not as subtle as usual,* Leslie mused, then reminded herself that she'd never been a great fan of Brad's. Even before he'd launched his playboy routine, she'd found him far too pretentious for her taste.

"Well, if there's anything...."

"She'll be fine. Take my word for it."

He sent her on her way with a brotherly kiss on the cheek. Once in her car, Leslie quickly wiped it off and pulled out of the drive, reluctantly concluding that she'd done her best. Yes, she was still worried about Diane. But if Diane didn't want her help and Brad didn't want her help, she could only butt in so far. Besides, she was suddenly in the mood for thinking about Oliver.

As she drove home, she thought of how much more handsome he was than Brad. While she lingered on her living-room sofa over a cup of tea, she thought of how much more sincerely he came across. When she climbed into bed with a book, she thought of how he, and he alone, electrified her senses. Finally, despairing of concentration, she turned out the light and, setting doubts aside, gave herself up to dreams of how beautiful the coming weekend would be.

UNFORTUNATELY HER DREAMS were to remain unfulfilled. Leslie had barely stepped foot in the house after work on Thursday when the phone rang. She nearly panicked. Her relief at finding that it wasn't Oliver calling to cancel on her was short-lived.

It was Brad, in a state of panic himself. "You've got to get over here, Leslie! I don't know what to do!" Gone was all pretense of composure. He sounded frantic.

Leslie's stomach lurched. "What is it, Brad? What's happened?"

"She spent the day in her room. When I got home a little while ago I found that she'd been on a silent rampage."

"What are you talking about?"

"Her scissors. She's taken her scissors to the sheets, the pillows, the drapes, the clothes...it's a mess!"

Images of destruction had begun to form in Leslie's mind's eye. "Calm down, Brad," she said, trying desperately to stay that way herself. "What's she doing now?"

"That's the problem. Now she's in the dining room breaking dishes. She just stands there throwing them on the floor. When I try to stop her she aims at me! You've got to come over, Leslie! I can't seem to get through to her. Nothing I say registers. I don't know what to do!"

Nerves in a bundle, Leslie hung her head and pressed her fingers to her temple. "Okay, Brad." She thought aloud. "You stay there. I'll be right over. Did you call Tony?"

"What can Tony do? He's about as understanding as a bulldozer!"

Though on the surface brother and brother-in-law had always gotten along, Leslie could understand that Brad was, in his way, intimidated by Tony. "Okay. I'll take care of it. You watch Diane and make sure she doesn't hurt herself. I'm on my way."

Pressing the cut-off button, she punched out Tony's number. Since he'd taken over as president of the company, he'd also taken over as head of the family. It was the handing of power down a generation, with the senior Parish happy to hold no more than a purely titular position.

Leslie impatiently tapped her foot as the phone rang repeatedly. The receiver was finally lifted just as an angry voice finished its statement, "...always the one who has to!" The voice lowered. "Hello?"

"Mark?"

"It's Jason."

"Jason. This is Aunt Leslie. Is your dad home yet?"

"Yeah. Just a minute."

"Thanks."

She raised her eyes to the ceiling, praying he'd hurry. When she heard a rustle at the other end of the line, she readied herself.

"Leslie?"

"Tony! Thank heavens you're there."

"You sound hassled, Les. What's up?"

"It's Di. Brad just called. She's gotten worse."

"How . . . worse?"

"Violent."

"Violent? *Diane?*"

As calmly as she could, Leslie related what Brad had told her. "I'm going over there now. Brad doesn't have the foggiest as to what to do. Not that I do, but she needs *something*." When Tony remained silent, she prodded. "What do you think? Should we call someone? I mean, I'm not thrilled with the idea, but I'm nervous. It's fine and dandy to overlook strange behavior in the hopes it will go away, but when strange turns violent, it's scary."

Tony hesitated for only a minute. "I agree. Listen, I'll get on the phone. You go on over and see what you can do. I'll meet you there as soon as I can."

"Thanks, Tony," Leslie said, then quickly hung up and reached for the coat she'd discarded just moments before. Tony was good at this type of thing—identifying resources, sifting through to find the cream of the crop. She felt assured that he'd come up with a qualified professional to treat Diane.

The scene at Brad and Diane's was gut-wrenching.

"Where is she?" Leslie asked the subdued Brad who answered the door. His face was pale, his hair disheveled. He bore a look of shock; she couldn't help but wonder how he'd managed to be so ignorant of Diane's mental state that he hadn't seen this coming. Then she chided herself for her insensitivity. The man's wife was falling apart. Cad he might be, yet he had a right to be upset.

"She's in the den," he said grimly.

Leslie glanced toward the dining room. Even from where she stood she could see shards of fine white china littering the oak floor and overflowing onto the rug. She frowned and looked around, listening. "She's quiet?"

"She ran out of plates. And steam, I guess. She's just sitting there crying."

Thrusting her coat toward Brad, she headed that way without a word. On the threshold, she faltered. Diane sat, a petite form in a long white robe, curled in an over-size armchair in the corner. Head bent, one hand to her face and another tucked against her waist, she was a pathetic figure.

"Di," Leslie whispered in agony, leaving the door and quickly crossing the room. She knelt before her sister's chair and placed her hands on its arms for support. "Di, what is it? Di?"

Diane's sobbing was quiet and internal, far different from the violent behavior she'd exhibited earlier. When she continued to cry, Leslie coaxed her gently.

"Diane, it's me. Leslie. I want to talk. Come on. Say something."

Very slowly Diane raised tear-drenched eyes. Time seemed to fly back to the day she'd been eighteen and had lost the most important gymnastic competition of her life. She looked crushed.

"Leslie?" she murmured in a small, high voice.

As though Diane were one of her preschoolers rather than actually two years older than her, Leslie reached up to tuck a long brown wave of hair from her cheek. "What is it, Di?" she asked gently. "What's bothering you?"

"Oh, Les," Diane began with a new rush of tears,

"I've...made a mess of...things. I've really...blown it."

Leslie took her hand and held it firmly. "No, you haven't. Everything can be put to rights."

Diane was shaking her head even as Leslie spoke. "No. No. You don't understand. It's...everything. I'm lousy at the office. They override every decision I make. I'm lousy here. He finds his pleasure everywhere else—"

"No, Di—"

"It's true!" Diane cried, eyes suddenly flashing. "I hate him! I hate all of them!"

"Shhhh. You don't mean that—"

"I do!"

For a minute Leslie just rubbed the back of her sister's hand. If Diane were indeed four years old, she'd know what to say. Even now her temptation was to acknowledge that she had simply thrown one hell of a temper tantrum and now just needed a good talking to. But it wasn't that simple. Diane wasn't four; she was thirty-two. And her temper tantrum had involved acts that could easily have been harmful to herself. Then there had been the days of depression beforehand.... Where was Tony? Where was help?

"You may feel that way now, Di, but you're angry."

"I'm...not...angry...." She dissolved into tears again.

Rising from her kneeling position, Leslie perched on the arm of the chair and tried to put her arm around her sister. When Diane resisted, burrowing more deeply into the cushions, Leslie had to settle for her hand again.

"Can I get you anything? A glass of wine? Warm milk?"

Crying softly, Diane simply shook her head.

"How about lying down?"

"I...can't. The room's destroyed."

"You could lie down on the sofa here." She started to get up. "I'll get a blanket—"

"No! I . . . don't want . . . to lie down!"

Feeling totally inadequate in the role of therapist, Leslie patted her hand. "Okay, hon. We'll just sit here."

"You don't have . . . to stay. . . . "

"I know."

"I'm . . . such a burden. Now to you, too."

"You're not a burden," Leslie argued ever so softly and urgently. Her face bore a pained expression. She didn't think she'd ever seen such dire unhappiness, such raw despair as she now saw on her sister's face.

Then she glanced up and, in a wave of relief, saw Tony stride through the door. Her gaze fell again to Diane, and she wondered what her reaction would be to seeing him.

"Diane?" Tony said, hunkering down before her much as Leslie had done at first. "Are you all right?"

Diane looked up in alarm. "Tony! You . . . shouldn't be . . . here!" she cried between sobs, wrenching her hand from Leslie's to cover her face with it. "I don't want . . . you to see. . . . "

"Diane, I've brought someone with me. He'd like to talk to you."

Only then did Leslie look up, her expression hopeful in a desperate kind of way. Then she froze. Her eyes grew larger. Hopefulness yielded to confusion, creating such a whir of sounds in her head that she barely heard Tony's words.

"This is Dr. Ames, Diane. He's going to help you."

8

SHOCKED, LESLIE WATCHED as Tony straightened and moved aside to let Oliver take his place. Dr. Ames. *Dr. Ames?* The man in question shot her a somber glance before turning his attention to Diane.

"Hi, Diane," he said in a low, gentle voice. "Not feelin' great?"

Diane looked up, first at Tony, then Leslie, her tear-streaked face accusing them of betrayal. "What is this?" she whispered.

Leslie couldn't possibly have answered. She felt numb, as stunned as Diane. Tony chose not to answer. It was Oliver who came to the rescue.

"I'd like to help you."

"But...you're a...psych...."

"A psychiatrist. That's right." His voice was miraculously calm in light of the anguished expression he sent toward Leslie, who was far too busy comprehending his words to begin to see the pain accompanying them.

A psychiatrist? It had to be some kind of joke. This was Oliver of Homme Premier fame. Free heart. Golden boy. The man she'd once actually thought to be a gigolo. *Her* Oliver. His skin bore its familiar tan, his features their familiar shape. And the silver C behind his ear—it was there as well.

Yet something was different. Was it the tailored slacks he wore, or the blazer or shirt or tie? Was it the air of authority about him? But he'd had that even on St. Barts. Now, though, it was...professional.

Stupefied, Leslie raised glassy eyes to Tony, who was looking directly at her. Obviously feeling Diane to be in the best of hands, his concern had shifted. In an instant Leslie realized that he'd known all along. Of course. They played tennis together, didn't they? They were friends. Tony had known just whom to call tonight.

Feeling superfluous at the moment and badly in need of fresh air, Leslie stood abruptly and started for the door. But Oliver caught her arm. His voice was calm, his expression well schooled. Only his fingers, fiercely circling her wrist, betrayed the intensity of emotion within him.

"Why don't you wait in the other room," he ordered softly. "I'll be out to talk with you in a minute."

Releasing her hand he turned back to Diane, to all appearances having done nothing more than offer support to the distraught relative of his patient. Tony knew better. He followed Leslie out, leaving Oliver to deal with Diane.

Feeling on the verge of suffocation, Leslie ran to the front door and opened it. She stood gasping the cold air when Tony reached her.

"Leslie?"

She shot him a look of bewilderment, then looked back out at the driveway, a bleak winter scene.

"It's all right, Les. There's really nothing so terrible about a psychiatrist."

"A psychiatrist?" she echoed dumbly. "I can't believe it. He's a model. A handsome model."

"No, Les. He's a handsome psychiatrist who happens to model on the side."

"But I . . . he can't . . . I never . . . ." She shook her head in confusion and slumped sideways against the door.

"Come on in, Les. You'll catch cold."

"I've already had my cold. He took care of me. A doctor . . . damn!"

"It's really no big thing—"

"No big thing?" she exclaimed, turning the force of her upheaval on Tony. "That's easy for you to say! You weren't the one who spent the week with the guy! You weren't the one who believed his lies!" And he certainly wasn't the one who'd fallen in love. In deep pain, she turned her head. "He didn't tell me," she murmured. "All that, and he didn't tell me...."

Watching the agony his sister endured, Tony felt hamstrung. It would be so simple to tell her of Oliver's pain, but he'd promised his friend that he'd keep out of it. It was bad enough that the revelation had been forced upon them tonight; for that, too, Tony felt responsible. Too late he wondered if he might have been able to keep Leslie away from this house; unfortunately, at the time, he'd been more concerned with seeing that Diane was all right. Brad seemed useless. Even now he stood at the door of the den, his eyes downcast, his charm nonexistent.

"Come in from the cold, Les," Tony said again.

She looked up, uncomprehending at first, frowning in puzzlement. Then, as though suddenly given direction, she pushed off from the doorjamb and moved into the house, but only to put on the coat that Brad had dropped on a nearby chair.

Tony eyed her cautiously. "Where are you going?"

With her coat hanging open, she dug her keys from the pocket and turned to the door again. "Home." She felt numb and simply wanted time and space to consider what she'd learned.

"Wait, Les!. You can't leave!"

"Why not?"

"Diane. Diane needs you."

"Diane's got capable help. He *is* capable, I assume," she snapped sarcastically.

"The best. But she'll need our support, too."

"You stay here. And Brad's here, for what that's worth. I only know that I wouldn't be much good to her tonight." She was already outside and halfway down the steps.

"But Oliver said to wait—"

"Tell Oliver," she yelled on the run toward her car, "that I don't take orders from anyone! Least of all *him*!"

"Leslie . . . !"

But she had slammed the door and started the engine before he could say any more. He stood helplessly and watched as she whirled her car around and gunned from the drive, praying that she'd have the sense to slow down before she got herself killed. Glancing at his watch, he calculated the amount of time it would take for her to drive home. Then, vowing to call to make sure she was all right, he quietly closed the door and turned back toward the den.

Oliver had drawn a chair up close to Diane and continued to talk to her in a slow, soft reassuring manner. At Tony's return, he stood, squeezed her shoulder and walked to the door, where he gestured with his chin toward the hall. When Tony joined him there, he spoke in hushed tones.

"I think she's gotten the worst of it out of her system. She's tired and confused. I'll give her something to help her sleep." He glanced up briefly when Brad joined the conference, then swung his attention back to Tony. "Is there someone who can stay with her?" He frowned and looked around. "Where's Leslie?"

"She's gone home," Tony ventured hesitantly, at once aware of the way his friend's jaw tensed at the news.

Oliver thrust his fingers through his hair. "Swell," he muttered under his breath, then turned to Brad. "Your wife is upset. She'll need to rest and then talk with someone. I'll stay with her until she falls asleep. Can you get her to my office tomorrow morning?"

Unbelievably, Brad grew nervous. "You don't think she should be, uh, hospitalized?"

"No, I don't," Oliver decreed, his voice low and taut. "Hospitalization at this point would only upset her more."

"But what about what she's done?" Brad countered. "What if she wakes up and turns violent again?"

"She won't. She's let off the worst of the steam . . . and she's got our full attention. Now she needs our understanding and support."

"She doesn't want *me* to do anything for her," Brad went on in a sulking tone. "I tried before. She wouldn't let me near."

"That's because you're very much a part of her problem," Oliver stated with a decided lack of sympathy for the man who'd been so blind to his wife's worsening mental state. Tony had filled him in on the history of the Weitzes' married life, and though it wasn't Oliver's job to pass judgment, he couldn't deny his anger. Anymore than he could deny his need to get out of this house and go after Leslie. "Tony tells me you've got a housekeeper."

"Some help she is," Brad grumbled. "She's been hiding in the kitchen through all of this."

"Can I see her?"

"I guess so." With a parting glance of irritation toward the dining-room door, Brad stalked off toward the kitchen.

"Nice guy," Oliver couldn't help but observe.

"Yeah. But Diane loves him. At least she did."

"She still does or she wouldn't have gone off the deep end like this."

Tony grew more alert. "Has she, Oliver? What's the prognosis for this kind of thing?"

Oliver shrugged. "I've only talked with her for a few minutes. But between that and what you've told me, I think she's got very workable problems."

"You can help her?"

"In time." He frowned, his eyes clouding. "I just hope I'm the one to do it."

"Why not? You're the best."

He snorted. "Be that as it may, I happen to be emotionally involved with your *other* sister, and that fact could complicate my treating Diane." Hands in the pockets of his slacks, he crossed the hall to stand by the front bay window.

Tony was quickly by his side again. "Come on, Oliver. Don't make me go to someone else in a matter as sensitive as this."

Something in his voice, a note of urgency, pricked Oliver's curiosity. "Your family isn't big on psychiatry, is it?"

"Why do you say that?" Tony returned defensively.

"Because, among many families in your social stratum, psychiatrists have become standard fixtures. I'm surprised that none of you thought to call in someone earlier."

"We didn't want to interfere. We thought it was a matter between Diane and Brad. It wasn't until today that we realized how bad things were. Leslie's been trying to see Diane all week, but she'd put her off each time. . . ." When Oliver simply continued to stare expectantly at him, he scowled. "All right. We're not big on psychiatry. My mother was pretty unhappy during the last years of her life. We don't talk about it much, but I think we all agree that the guy she was seeing didn't do her much good."

"She was seeing a psychiatrist?" Leslie had never mentioned this. "Why?"

"Depression. Anger. Loneliness."

"With a husband and four kids?"

"It was the husband she wanted, and he was never around. What with business trips and all. . . ." He'd said enough, without elaborating on the "and all." "The kids could only fulfill certain needs. She had a slew of others that were never addressed."

"How did she die?"

"She didn't commit suicide, if that's what you're thinking. She had cancer. I think she just...gave up. Not much difference, I suppose."

Oliver was given no time to comment, for Brad returned with a shy-looking woman in tow. Introductions were made, at which point Oliver spoke kindly to the woman, asking her to check in on her mistress at intervals during the night. Diane was not to awaken alone. She was to be made comfortable and given food or drink or anything of the like that she wanted. And he was to be called if there was any further problem.

Returning to Diane, Oliver gave her a sedative and helped her upstairs to a bedroom at the opposite end of the house from the one she'd torn apart. All the while he talked quietly with her, demanding little, letting her speak as she wished. The housekeeper brought the glass of warm milk he'd requested; he supported Diane while she drank. Then, denying the gremlins that thudded impatiently inside him, he sat by her bedside until the sedative took effect, leaving only when he was sure she was asleep.

LESLIE WISHED SHE were out of it. Her mind was in a turmoil from which neither the sobering drive home nor her arrival at her own warm, familiar house nor a glass of her best and most mellow wine could rescue her. She picked up the mail, looked through it, put it down. She turned on the television, ran the gamut of channels, switched it off. She went to the refrigerator, stared at its contents, shut the door without touching a thing.

Wiping a single tear from her eye, she climbed the stairs to her bedroom and lay down in the dark. She felt hurt and tired, stretched taut by the emotions that gathered into a tight knot deep inside.

When the phone rang, she simply glared at it. Then it rang a second, a third and a fourth time and she realized that it might well be Brenda calling in concern about Diane.

"Hello?" she began cautiously, prepared to hang up if it was Oliver.

It was Tony. "Thank goodness," he breathed. "You got home all right."

"Of course I did," she answered in quiet relief, then growing irritation. "What could have happened?"

"The way you were driving, I wasn't sure."

"I'm all right."

"Are you?"

"Relatively speaking."

"He wasn't pleased that you'd left."

"Tough. How's Diane?"

"He took her to bed."

"Oh, great."

"He *brought her upstairs*. He gave her a sedative and said he'd talk with her until she drifted off."

"Then what?"

"Then he'll probably go after *you*."

Leslie scowled in frustration. "Then what does he have planned for Diane? One sedative and a good-night talk is hardly going to solve her problem."

"He'll see her in his office tomorrow."

"That's good of him."

"It is, given the fact that he's booked solid, and that he's got serious reservations about treating her, what with his relationship with you. Come on, Leslie. Ease up."

"Relationship with me," she muttered to herself. "*What* relationship? A relationship based on lies is nothing!"

Tony started to argue, then caught himself, fearing he'd only make things worse. "Listen," he said in his most placating tone, "Oliver will explain everything. I've got to run. I'll catch you later."

"Sure," Leslie murmured, hanging up the phone and lying back in the dark again. She didn't know how much time passed, only knew that she couldn't motivate herself to do anything but lie there and wonder how she'd managed to get hurt again. It hurt. It did hurt. As the numbness slowly wore off, the sting had begun.

When the front doorbell rang, she wasn't surprised. She'd known he would come. The male mind was very predictable when it came to bruised egos, and she'd bruised his with her refusal to hang around at Diane's house. No, it hadn't taken psychiatric wizardry to anticipate his move.

She lay in the dark listening. The bell rang again and again. When he began to pound on the thick wood, she simply turned onto her side and huddled in a tighter ball. When the back bell rang, again followed by knocking, she flipped onto the other side. She heard the vague echo of her name and found perverse satisfaction in his annoyance. His ego certainly was bruised; small solace for the tatters to which he'd reduced hers!

To her amazement, he gave up after several minutes. She grew more alert, listening closely for any sounds of his prowling outside. But what could she possibly hear? Her bedroom was on the second floor. It was the middle of winter. Snow blanketed the ground, providing a natural cushion for footsteps, while thick storm windows blocked out not only the cold but extraneous noise as well.

It was spooky, she had to admit, lying here, wondering if she was being stalked. She sat up to listen. Slipping quietly from the bed, she stood at the door. Everything was still. Had he left, the coward? Had he tossed in the towel so easily? Then it had been illusion, what she'd imagined he'd felt on St. Barts. Illusion and deception—all she detested.

A sound caught her ear and brought her instantly alert. A door shutting. In the kitchen? Then she heard footsteps and nearly panicked. Someone was in her house. Someone had broken in. The alarm . . . what had happened to the alarm? Had she actually forgotten to reengage it after she'd come in? Everything had been locked; she was sure of it. Hand on her thudding heart, she stood rooted to the spot, thinking she should call the police but waiting, waiting. . . .

"Leslie! Where are you? I know you're here!"

Her heart continued to thud, despite the wave of relief that swept over her. The footsteps came and went as he passed from area rugs to hardwood floors and back. He searched the living room, the dining room, the library, the den. On stocking feet she walked quietly from her bedroom door to the top of the stairs. Though the lower floor was bathed in light, she stood in darkness, waiting.

When Oliver reached the stairs and looked up, he saw her instantly. Hand on the end curl of the wood bannister, one foot on the lowest rung of the steps, he stared up at her for a moment.

"Come on down, Leslie," he said evenly, his manner tautly reined. "We have to talk."

"How did you get in?" Her voice was as tight as his.

"Through the garage. The lock on the inner door was easy to pick."

"That's breaking and entering, Oliver. Another of your surprise talents?" She hadn't moved, finding small comfort in the advantage of her raised position.

"The fact is," he snarled, whipping off his overcoat and throwing it over the bannister, "that it was a lousy lock. You should be better protected than that. I'm surprised no one's broken in before."

"Someone has. I have an alarm system."

"It did one hell of a job just now."

"It wasn't on."

"Swell! Your insurance company would be real pleased! So you're one of those who feels that the little sticker on the front window is enough to scare away a thug?"

"It didn't scare *you* away. What would you have done if the whole system had gone off, and you'd found yourself surrounded by cops? It's hooked in to the police station, you know."

"I would have told them the truth. And I certainly would have had your attention."

"Oh, you've got my attention, all right," she spat. "You've had that since the first time I found you in my bed. Thing is that I could get you for perjury."

Oliver simmered. "Come downstairs, Leslie. I can't talk standing here like this staring up into the dark. I'd like to see your face."

Her fingers tightened on the wood railing. "Why? So you can gauge my reactions and gear your words accordingly? So you can analyze my frame of mind and plot your counterattack? So you can—"

"Leslie! Get down here!" he thundered, then swore softly and lowered his voice. "Please. It's been a long day for both of us. I'm tired and no more wild about this turn of events than you are."

"I bet you're not," she bounded on, driven by the anguish festering within. "I bet you'd have liked to have kept the charade going a while longer. Fun."

Oliver shot her a withering stare, reached up to loosen his tie, then turned and headed for the den. In her mind's eye, Leslie saw him approach the bar, remove a glass, open the small refrigerator below, extract the same bottle she had earlier and uncork it. Only when she heard the refrigerator door close with a thud did she very slowly start down the stairs.

He met her at its bottom holding two glasses, his own and the one he'd refilled for her. Head high, she took it from him without a word and padded softly into the living room. It was a larger room, not quite as intimate as the den and, for that very reason, never a favorite of hers. On this occasion, she mused, it would serve just fine. She needed the space. She also needed four-inch spikes; she felt suddenly much smaller and more insignificant than she had before. It took all her courage to settle calmly into the armchair and tip her head at its most arrogant angle toward Oliver.

She waited in silence, determined to do nothing to put him at ease. For ease was the last thing she felt. Looking at Oliver, vitally aware of his very presence in her home, she felt as though she were being torn apart. Strange, when Joe had come to her apartment that last time, she'd felt angry and strong and vindictive. Now, though, angry and vindictive were simply for show, while strong was nonexistent. What *did* she feel? She ached—inside, outside, everywhere.

Oliver took several gulps of wine, then tugged his tie looser and unbuttoned the top collar of his shirt. Anchoring one hand in the pocket of his slacks, he looked down at her. "I was going to tell you this weekend," he said quietly.

"Were you." It wasn't a question, rather a statement whose blatant mockery was quickly punished by the piercing arrow of his gaze.

"I would have told you as soon as we arrived in the mountains, once I'd isolated you from the world so you wouldn't be able to run out of the house and barrel off in your car. That was a dumb thing to do, Leslie!"

"That's strange." She gritted her teeth against the

hurt. "I thought it was pretty smart. I wasn't needed there. Diane was well taken care of."

"And what about us?"

"We were well taken care of, too."

"Well taken care of . . . as in finished?" he asked, his voice grating. "Not quite."

She sipped her wine without tasting a drop. Then she took another sip, a larger one in search of the inner warmth that totally eluded her. She drew her legs up under her and wrapped her arms about her waist. "I think so," she murmured. "You've ruined everything."

"Only if you decide that I have," he countered firmly. His jaw was clenched, his shoulders rigid. "I'm not Joe Durand, Leslie. I did nothing immoral. And I didn't set out to hurt you. That was the last thing I wanted to do."

"You lied."

"I never lied."

"You said you were a model. Not a psychiatrist. A model."

"I am a model. You've seen my work. I pose every so often just for the fun of it. And I never said I *wasn't* a psychiatrist. I just—" his voice lowered "—didn't say that I was."

"And that's not lying?"

"Technically, no."

"Then you're splitting hairs, Oliver. You let me go on believing that . . . that . . . oh, what the hell." Eyes moist, she looked away and took a fast drink of her wine.

"Go on."

And give him the satisfaction of seeing how badly she ached? "No."

"You disappoint me," he taunted. "You're a woman of strong opinions. You mean to say that you've suddenly gone private with them? Where's the woman who asked point-blank why I'd choose to spend a quiet week at her Caribbean villa rather than live it up at a nearby hotel?"

"Maybe she's wary of the answers. Maybe she knows not to trust them anymore." Finding small satisfaction in seeing Oliver wince, she once again sank into a dark, brooding silence. Bowing her head, she didn't see him set his wine down on the nearby coffee table. Only when his hands settled on the arms of her chair did she grow aware of the large body bent over her.

"That's bull," his voice rumbled near her ear. "Her pride's been hurt, and she's vulnerable and in love—"

Leslie snapped her head up. "She is not!"

"No?" he hummed, his lips near her cheek.

Momentarily unable to function, she closed her eyes. He was close and warm and beckoning. His smell, clean and natural even at the end of the day, titillated her senses. All week she'd waited to be with him. She wanted him so badly. . . .

"No," she whispered, reinforcing the lie. If he could do it, so could she.

"I love you, Leslie," he murmured, his own eyes closed, his own senses absorbing her closeness. All week he'd waited to be with her. He wanted her so badly. . . .

"No!" she screamed, taking him by surprise and bolting past him. Oblivious to the slosh of wine over her hand, she ran to the fireplace and turned to face him. "No!" she cried, suddenly shaking all over. "I don't want to hear it! You had plenty of time to say it before. You had plenty of time to say everything before. Now it's too late. I can't believe any of it!"

"Leslie—" He started toward her.

"Don't come near me!" she yelled, cringing against the marble. When he continued forward, she tried to escape to the side, only to have her shoulders caught in the vise of his hands. "Let me go! I don't want you touching me!"

"You'll hear me out," he growled, then grunted when her foot hit his shin. Rather than releasing her, he slid his hands to her upper arms for better leverage, then with one hand relieved her of her endangered wineglass. "Childish, Les. Really childish."

"You must be used to it," she gritted, trying to push against his arms and free herself. "You're the expert on temper tantrums." She twisted and turned, but to no avail. Even when she brought her knee up, she was thwarted. Anticipating her ploy, he easily blocked the move.

"You told me about that little trick once before. Remember? You shouldn't have tipped your hand."

"I didn't think I'd need to try it on you. Let . . . me . . . go!"

"No way," he growled, all but carrying her to the sofa. "You're going to hear me out if it kills us both."

"And then where will Diane be? Where will your other precious patients be? Where will the adoring public in love with the Homme Premier man be?"

Having shoved her into an upholstered corner, he stood over her, his hands on the sofa arm and back, barring her escape. "I don't give a good goddamn about anyone but you. And you will listen to what I have to say! Now, do I have to restrain you, or do you think you can try to behave yourself?"

"I am behaving myself," she said quietly.

He stared at her suddenly still form for a minute, then straightened. Taking a long, ragged breath, he walked to the far end of the room, turned back toward her, and tucked both hands in his pockets.

"When Tony suggested I spend a week on St. Barts, it sounded like a super idea. I was tired. I needed a vacation. When he told me about you and his little joke, I wasn't deterred. It sounded like fun, entirely harmless. Tony said you were the independent sort and that you'd

probably go about your business as though I wasn't
even there. Other than sharing laughs that first day. I
didn't expect a thing."

"Got slightly more than that, didn't you," she murmured morosely.

"Slightly. I didn't expect an adorable purple elf with a
whopper of a head cold bounding into my bedroom to
wake me up."

"Adorable?" She screwed up her face. "As in puppy?
Something you trick into fetching slippers solely for the
sake of a stale biscuit?"

His tone softened. "Adorable as in fresh and pretty."

"Come off it, Oliver! I was sweaty and hot." The last
thing she needed was his sweet-talking, given her pecu-
liar susceptibility to it.

"Sweaty and hot, then fresh and pretty. . .and needing my care." He came several steps closer. "You don't
know what that does to a man in this day and age, to
feel needed."

She eyed him skeptically. "You're needed all the time!
Look at the way Diane needed you, not to mention the
crew of unhappy people who must have brooded
around Manhattan while you were away."

"Professionally, fine. I was talking personally. And on
a personal level, it's nice to feel needed once in a while."

"Polishes that image of the macho protector?"

His lips thinned. "The image of the macho protector is
nothing compared to the one you're trying to project of
the hard-bitten independent woman. Sarcasm doesn't
become you, Les."

She had no smart retort. He was right. She didn't care
for her tone any more than he did, and the fact that she
was merely lashing out in anger did nothing to sweeten
the bitter taste in her mouth. She dropped her gaze to
the fingers clenched in her lap and listened as Oliver
went on in a softer tone.

"You saw me as the man from the ad. To tell you the truth, I kind of enjoyed it." When she raised her head and took a breath to protest, he held up a hand. "No, no, Leslie. I'm not making fun of you. It was from a selfish standpoint that I enjoyed it. It was a new image for me. Believe it or not," he said less surely, "I needed that."

"I don't believe it," she said, but without sarcasm. She was puzzled. It didn't make sense. "What could possibly be wrong with being a psychiatrist?"

"Do you like psychiatrists?"

"No...but my situation is different. And my bias is strictly emotional. From an intellectual point of view, I respect the fact that you've had to make it through med school to get into psychiatry."

"Thank you," he drawled with a touch of sarcasm of his own, then grew more firm. "But most people don't think of that when they meet me. They think of how eager I must be to hear their problems, how good I must be at reading their minds, how neurotic I must be myself. When a psychiatrist meets people, they usually fall into two categories. There are those who treat him like he's got the plague, who are aloof, who won't go near him for fear that he'll see something deep inside that they'd rather hide. And there are those who flock to him and tell him everything." His face contorted. "Do you have any idea how boring that can be?"

"Don't you like your work?"

"I love my work...*when I'm working*. Not twenty-fours hours a day. Not when I want to relax. Not when I go to parties or dinners or the theater." In vehemence, his brows drew together. "It's damned frustrating to be constantly labeled. In the first place, I don't identify with many of my more eccentric colleagues. In the second place, *I'm a man*." His voice had risen steadily. Suddenly, as though a bubble inside him had popped, he spoke more softly. "At any rate, that was why I didn't jump to correct your misconception when you assumed that I was a model. It was my vacation. What better way to escape reality than by taking on a new identity?"

His manner was so sincere that Leslie could almost believe him. Almost...but not quite. He'd seemed so sincere about everything before. She'd believed then—and felt humiliated now.

"But you let me say so many things," she argued with a surge of embarrassment, "things about women and action and—" she tried to remember them all "—and aging. I even implied that your parents might be ashamed of your work."

To her relief, Oliver didn't laugh. "And everything I answered was honest. My parents are proud of what I do. And I do model, Leslie. Even though it's a hobby, I get a significant amount of money for it. I don't stick around long enough to see the glamorous side. You imagined that; I simply did nothing to disillusion you." He took a deep breath and walked to the fireplace, where he stood with one elbow on the mantel, one foot raised on the hearth. His gaze raked the cold, ash-strewn grates. "Modeling is an escape for me. To spend an afternoon doing something as light as that is refreshing. I need it from time to time."

His voice seemed to hover in the air, then drop into a chasm of silence. Leslie tried to find fault with his reasoning, but couldn't. Oliver tried to find reasoning for his fault, but couldn't.

"I should have told you everything."

"You should have. Why didn't you?"

He looked at her then, his expression one of vulnerability. Not wanting to be affected, she lowered her eyes. But his words came to her nonetheless, accompanied by a note of urgency. "Because at first I enjoyed the role I was playing. Then, as the week went on, it grew stale. And about the time I realized that you were something very special to me, I got wind of your obsession with honesty."

"So why didn't you say something?"

"*I was scared!*" he bellowed, feeling angry and frustrated and embarrassed, just as Leslie had felt.

She wanted to doubt him. "You? Scared?"

"Yes," he answered somberly. "Me, scared. I wanted you. I needed you. You seemed to be everything I'd waited thirty-nine years for. I felt as though we'd gotten off to such a good start. I didn't know what to do. On the one hand, I didn't want you to know I was a psychiatrist. It's so...complicated sometimes. A model—that's simpler. On the other hand, I knew you'd be upset if I didn't tell you." He took a breath, then threw up a hand in frustration. "It was the old story. With each day that passed, it got more difficult. The longer the deception went on, the more I feared confessing to it. And in the end, the joke was on me. By the time we were ready to return to New York, I knew I loved you...and though I hated myself for having deceived you, I didn't know how in hell to correct the error without the risk of losing you completely."

He swallowed hard. His hand gripped the mantel until his knuckles were white. Gazing at Leslie, he hated himself all the more for having put that look of misery on her face. Somehow, some way, he had to convince her of his love.

"I tried to tell you, Leslie. Several times as the week went on, I tried to tell you. But you wouldn't let me, and I was happy enough not to push. There were times when I wondered if you knew. Once when you kiddingly called me Dr. Ames, another time when you begged me not to analyze things to death." His voice grew deeper. "Do you remember that time? We were on the terrace. . . ." He started to move toward her but she quickly rose from the sofa and crossed the room to stand at the window with her back to him. In tailored wool slacks, a sweater and blouse, she looked every bit the successful businesswoman, every bit the caring teacher, every bit the woman he loved.

"I remember a comment you made," she began in a distant voice, her mind, too, back on St. Barts, "when I thought Tony had paid you to give me a good time. You laughed and said that nobody paid you for your time in chunks like that. I suppose I should have wondered what you meant, but I assumed you were talking of modeling. Deep down under all that wariness, I was so. . .so anxious to believe." She shook her head in dismay. "What is it about me?" she asked herself. "After Joe, I swore I'd never be taken in. One week with you. . .and bam, I'm blind all over again."

Oliver came up from behind and stood at her side without touching her. "Love is blind," he said, casting a sad smile her way. "Haven't you heard that saying?"

She gave a meager excuse for a laugh. "Yeah. Dumb, isn't it?"

"Not dumb at all. I let love blind me to your need for the truth. I let it convince me to leave well enough alone." His voice took on a husky timbre. "I do love you, Leslie. And if you weren't so hurt and angry I think you'd admit that you love me, too."

"But I am hurt and angry," she argued, the proof of her words in her large violet eyes, which were open and pleading. "I feel. . .betrayed."

"Aw, Les," he moaned, "I haven't betrayed you." He reached out to touch her cheek, but she flinched and he let his hand drop. "Everything about me is the same as it was. Psychiatrist and model, they're one and the same. If you could love the model, why not the psychiatrist?"

"I didn't love the model!" she cried, grasping at the

one illusion that might save her from the power Oliver had. For she felt it now—the need to touch him, to hold him and be held, to find oblivion in the fire of his passion. "I got...carried away by the romance of the island. That was what it was. Nothing more."

His gaze narrowed knowingly. "Is that why you were so quiet during the trip home? Is that why you so readily agreed to spend the weekend with me? Is that why you gave yourself to me with such abandon, why you'd do it again if I took you upstairs now? You 'don't sleep around.' Remember?"

Leslie's heart began to knot up. Whether it was his skill as a psychiatrist or simply that of a very perceptive man, he asked pointed questions. "You're good in bed," she heard herself say in a voice far cooler than the caldron heating within. "And I needed the escape. Maybe you weren't the only one trying to flee an image," she said, the words coming fast as the ideas formed. "Maybe I needed to shake the image of the down-to-earth schoolteacher for the week. Maybe I did have a ball. Maybe I was truly sorry to see my vacation end. Maybe my acceptance of your invitation for the weekend was nothing more than a wish to escape for two final days. Maybe I was playing a role, too."

She'd hit home. Oliver stood suddenly straighter. "I don't believe you."

"That's a shame. Funny...it seems to be a hazard of trips such as ours. When two people play for a week, it's hard to know afterward what's for real." Given strength by self-deception, she turned and headed for the front door. "I think you ought to leave," she said without looking at him. "The game is over."

"Not by a long shot!" Oliver exclaimed, coming from behind to whirl her around. "I don't believe a word you say. I know you, Leslie. I can see inside."

She pulled her arm from his grip. "Then you've got a

double problem. Because if you want me to believe that, I'll have to believe all those stereotypes about psychiatrists. And if I do, I won't want to be around you. I've got secrets, just like everyone else. And I don't like the idea of being transparent." She took the few remaining steps toward the door and stood with her hand on the knob for support. Her legs felt like rubber. "Now are you going to leave, or do I call the cops and report a breaking and entering?" She crinkled up her nose in echo of her heart. "Wouldn't be good for the image, Ol. Either of them."

For a minute he stood staring at her. Though he hadn't believed a word she'd said, his claims to that effect had only hardened her. There had to be another approach, one that would be more successful. Unfortunately, he couldn't think straight. His insides were being chewed up; every bit of his energy was needed simply to keep his cool. Almost as an afterthought he remembered his overcoat on the bannister. Head down, back straight, he retrieved it, then returned to the door as Leslie opened it.

"This isn't the end, Leslie."

"I think so," she whispered, suffering behind a mask that barely hid her pain.

He simply shook his head. Daring to touch her because he needed to so badly, he lifted a hand to her face. When she tried to draw back, he anchored his fingers all the more firmly in her hair. "No, Les. What we had on St. Barts was unique. Most people go through a lifetime in a futile search for it. I'm done searching. All I have left to do is to prove that you are, too." He let his thumb drift ever so gently along her cheek to her lips. She wanted to pull back, to shake it off, to do anything but admit to herself how much she craved him. But she was rooted to the spot.

Again he shook his head, this time with a smile to

match the tenderness of his touch. "We found a special something down there, and I'll be damned if I'm going to let it go."

For a split second, she thought he would take her in his arms. Her eyes widened. She swallowed hard. But while she was still trying to decide whether or not to fight, he dropped his hand, stepped away to put on his overcoat and left.

She stood in the doorway until his car was out of sight, then went upstairs and cried herself to sleep.

9

It was a long two weeks before Leslie heard from Oliver again, two weeks rehashing all that had been said and done between them, two weeks of soul-searching. At first she'd been constantly on her guard, wondering when or where he'd show up...for she was sure he would show up. She'd seen that look of determination in his eye when he'd spoken of the special something he'd found, and her feminine intuition told her to beware.

At the start there was anger, anger that Oliver had deceived her, anger that she'd fallen for his ruse. And there was the hurt of betrayal. Yes, they had had a special something, but it had been built on delusion and was now destroyed.

The pity of it was that she'd wanted it, too, that special something. She couldn't deny it any more than she could deny that the mere thought of Oliver set her heart to beating with a vigor it lacked at other times.

Oh, yes, she'd wanted it. Before she'd ever gone to St. Barts she'd been aware of a lack in her life. She'd been restless and searching. Hadn't she debated going back to school, or worse, joining the corporation? But either of those options would have been stopgap measures for an ailment that went far deeper. She loved her work as it was. What was missing was a man, a home, children of her own. She wanted a relationship, a closeness, a warmth. She wanted love. She was thirty now; hadn't she waited long enough?

A special something. She had, indeed, found it on St.
Barts. Illusion though it might have been, it had been
divine while it lasted. Somehow in comparison the rest
of her life paled dramatically.

By the end of the first week much of the anger and
hurt had filtered away, replaced by an overwhelming
sadness. She wanted to believe everything Oliver had
told her that last night at her house, but she couldn't.
She was afraid. . .afraid of trusting, then of being hurt
all over again. What they'd once had had been so good;
she felt as though she were mourning the loss of a limb
or an ideal or a dearly beloved friend.

And she was lonely. So very lonely. Even during the
hours she spent at one or another of the centers, she
ached. There was some solace in the fact that Diane appeared to be responding to Oliver's ministrations.
Though Leslie was unable to shake the vision of destruction at the Weitzes' house, regular phone calls to Tony,
then to Diane herself, assured her of progress on that
front. It was Brenda, however, who systematically
homed in on Leslie's own malady.

"You sound down, Leslie," she commented during
one evening's call.

"I'm worried about Di. You know that."

"And that's all?"

"Isn't it enough?"

"What about Oliver?"

Leslie stiffened, startled. "What about him?"

"Tony told me—"

"He had no business doing that!"

"He's your brother. He's worried."

"I told him I'd be all right."

"You don't sound it."

"Please, Bren. I don't want to argue."

But Brenda was insistent. "Is he very special. . .this
Oliver?"

Very special? Ironic choice of words. For an instant Leslie wondered whether Brenda wasn't in cahoots with the man himself, then she chalked it up to coincidence. "Yes," she sighed wearily. "He is."

"Then give, Leslie. Give a little."

She'd already given her heart. What was left? "Brenda . . ." she warned.

"Okay, but just try."

"I'm trying, I'm trying," Leslie grumbled, and indeed she was; she was trying to envision her future, but it remained a muddle. Thoughts of Oliver tore at her endlessly. *Classic withdrawal*, she told herself. Persevere, and she'd be fine. But the ache persisted, and by the end of the second week she'd begun to despair.

Then the kitten arrived. She'd just gotten home when the doorbell rang. For an instant she stood frozen, wondering whether this was the time Oliver had chosen to pop back into her life. But it was a delivery truck on the drive, leaving a small brown-wrapped box in her hand when it drove away.

An F.A.O. Schwarz package? She had no idea. Then she peeled back the wrapping and unearthed the sweetest hand-sized toy kitten she'd seen . . . since . . . since she was seven and her own just like it had gone to the laundry and never returned. Her vision blurred as she stared at the tiny silver button in its ear. Steiff. And its name. Jigs. She smiled and sniffed and shook her head. Then, hands trembling, she reached into the box and extracted the card buried therein.

"Not a puppy to chase and fetch, but a kitten to purr and stretch and thrive on attention. I'd even indulge it its occasional bristling. All my love, Oliver."

Collapsing on a nearby chair with the kitten pressed to her heart and her head buried against her arm, she burst into tears. How could he remember such a small thing as that? How could he do this to her?

But he had. He'd sent her a teaser, then nothing. Another week passed without a word. Staring at the kitten each night, picking it up in her hands and holding it, knowing that Oliver had to have done the same when he'd bought it, she felt all the sadder, all the more lonely.

Predictably, with time, she grew used to thinking of Oliver as a psychiatrist. Unpredictably, given her annoyance that he should be something other than what she'd been led to expect, she grew curious. From model to psychiatrist—it was quite a switch. When she'd been on St. Barts she'd imagined what his life as a model was like. She'd never asked for details, feeling foreign enough, intimidated enough, to be wary of asking. He'd volunteered little. As she reflected on it, she realized that those few times she'd asked him questions he'd deftly turned the conversation around. At the time she'd simply thought him to be all the more modest, all the more attentive to her. Now she realized that his attentiveness had probably been not only habitual probing, but a diversionary tactic as well.

To think of him now as a psychiatrist conjured up quite a different picture of the way he spent his days. Rather than being in a studio, perhaps wearing a terry robe that he'd shrug off when it was time to climb into bed for the shooting of something akin to the Homme Premier ad, he'd be in an office, dressed in conservative slacks and shirt, tie and blazer, much as he'd been dressed when he'd come to Diane's house that night. Tony said he was skilled; indeed Diane appeared to have gotten a temporary handle on the more erratic of her emotions. Tony said he was busy. Leslie pictured him behind his desk, leaning far back in a chair, his long fingers steepled against his lips as he listened intently to his patient's words, interjecting questions or suggestions, concentrating fully on that one individual until the end of the hour, when, like clockwork, the guard would change.

To each patient he would seem all-attentive, fully engrossed. That would be part of his skill, making the patient feel wanted. Just as Leslie had felt wanted, and needed, and loved.

No sooner had she chased that thought from her mind than her curiosity went to work again. She wondered what time he went to work in the morning, when he got home at night, what he did evenings and on weekends. He'd obviously been free enough to invite her away. But certainly he had a social life, and most certainly it would be of a different class from that of a full-time model. Ironically, she assumed it would be similar to the kind of social life her family knew. Oliver appeared to be successful. He lived in Manhattan, had a place in the Berkshires, had been able to easily swing a trip to St. Barts, not to mention the beautiful gold necklace she wore, yes, every day. No doubt he lived well. No doubt he was part of that same social world she'd sworn off so long ago. . . .

As the days passed, she was prone to abrupt mood swings, high one minute and low the next. She'd miss Oliver with all her heart, then be glad he was gone. She'd be relieved he wasn't a model, then sad it should be so. She'd be proud to think of him as a psychiatrist, then furious at the way he'd so skillfully manipulated her mind. She'd be angry then contrite, indignant then forgiving. But through it all she was confused. Her future seemed more in limbo than ever before. She simply didn't know where she wanted to go, and the unsureness of it all gnawed at her constantly.

By the end of the fourth week, the unbuttoned ear of the small stuffed kitten had begun to show the imprint of her thumb. Much as she wished it weren't so, Oliver was never far from her thoughts. With March nearing an end, spring wouldn't be long. And spring, well, spring was a time for birth and brightness and love.

Had he had that in mind the day he sent the vase filled with violets? Violets . . . not drooping as she'd been that first day she'd arrived on St. Barts, but fresh and moist and gay. Had he known how desperately she'd needed word from him?

Her hand shook as she read the card written in the now-familiar bold scrawl. "I couldn't resist. I'll never see a violet without thinking of you. Care for them . . . please?" It was signed, "Love, Oliver."

She was more rattled than ever. Though ecstatic to receive his gifts, she was terrified to read too much into them. Worse, she was appalled at how much she wanted to read into them. She was wary and elated, distrustful and optimistic, and very much afraid of being hurt again.

Determined to view the violets as nothing more than a token, she put them in the center of her bright kitchen table and tried to go about her business as usual. She went to work each day at one of the centers, invariably brought paperwork home to do at night, had a pleasant if uninspiring dinner-date with a college professor she'd dated from time to time, spoke to Tony and Brenda, met Diane for lunch.

And the violets remained on her table. She gave them fresh water. She misted them. She recut their stems. She withered a little as each delicate face fell, dried up and had to be removed from the bunch. With no more than four or five flowers left, the vase began to look as lonely as she felt.

Then, on a rainy Wednesday evening that just happened to be April Fool's Day, Leslie came home from work to find a puddle of water accumulating in her basement frighteningly close to the furnace. Tired and discouraged, she was trying to get the sump pump going when the doorbell rang. Struggling frantically, she poked and pinched in vain. Then the bell rang a second time. Swearing at the stubborn machine, she brushed off her hands as she ran up the stairs.

The house, a brick Tudor, had an inner door, a small foyer, then a thicker outer door with multiple locks. Dashing through the first door, she stood on tiptoe at the second to peer out its single window. She was saved! Flipping the locks, she opened the door.

Standing in the cover of the meager overhang was Oliver. His hair glistened; his raincoat was wet. Collar up, he was hunched over as though trying to protect himself from the rain.

Without a pause she stood aside to let him step quickly in out of the rain. His breathing came fast; he must have dashed from the car.

"Hi," he said, shaking out his sleeves. "Man, is it pouring! Listen, I'm sorry to barge in on you like this, but I was worried you wouldn't see me unless I took you by surprise—"

"Thank heavens you're here, Oliver! Do you know anything about sump pumps?" She reached up to help him out of his coat.

"Excuse me?"

"Sump pumps!" She hung the coat to drip on the tall brass coat stand, then led the way into the house and directly toward the basement door. "Do you know how they work...or what's wrong with them when they don't?" She was taking the stairs at a clip, calling back over her shoulder to the bemused figure following her lead. "I can't get the thing to work and my basement's beginning to flood and if the water keeps coming in the furnace is going to be knocked out and then I'll be without heat and—"

"Keep still for a minute while I take a look."

Oliver hunkered down and peered into the small hole

of the compact piece of machinery that was barely
above the water line. Shrugging out of his blazer and
handing it to her, he rolled up his shirt sleeve, then
reached in to locate a part here, to jiggle a part there, to
fiddle with still a third, while Leslie looked on.

"I can't believe this is happening!" she exclaimed. "I
have a service that comes in twice a year to check both
the furnace and the pump. They assured me both were
fine. What do you think?" she asked, anxiously clutching his blazer. "Should I call the plumber?"

"I think," he grunted, reaching lower to tug at a lever
that momentarily resisted him, "that the guy simply had
the thing turned off. It's stuck. Wait. . . . There." Sure
enough, with a final forceful tug, Oliver had the pump
started. Removing his hand from the water, he shook it,
then stood.

"It wasn't turned on," Leslie stated as though any fool
should have known it right off the bat. With an expression of exasperation, she shook her head. "Terrific April
Fool's Day prank. . . . Here, let me get you a towel." She
would have escaped up the stairs had Oliver not caught
her hand.

"The towel can wait. I can't." He drew her toward
him.

The basement was gray, lit by a sole bare bulb hanging over their heads like mistletoe. Leslie looked up at
Oliver then, and in an instant was hit by the fact of his
presence. *He was here.* He had come. Or was he nothing
more than a tall, dark and handsome April Fool's Day
mirage?

"Heeey, don't look so stricken," he whispered. "I'm
only going to kiss you." And kiss her he did, with one
large hand curved to her throat, the other arm around
her back holding her closer.

Leslie was stunned. In a matter of seconds, every one
of the emotions with which she'd been wrestling for five

weeks declared war. She loved him, she didn't. She needed him, she didn't. She trusted him, she didn't. She wanted him, she didn't. But . . . she did.

His lips felt wonderful on hers, bringing back thoughts of warmer, more carefree days on a distant Caribbean isle. His arms were strong, his body large and hard and just right to lean upon. Any thought Leslie might have had of denying her physical attraction to him was negated by the helplessness of her response. She needed to feel the hungry movement of his mouth, needed to respond to him for just that minute, just that minute . . . until sanity slowly returned. Only then did she put her palms to his chest and exert the gentle force that would speak for her.

Oliver instantly released her lips and buried his in her hair. Both of his arms circled her now, hugging her tightly for a minute. "Oh, Leslie, I've wanted to do that night after night," he whispered, then loosened his hold as she'd requested.

Looking up, Leslie met the same warm brown eyes that had so enchanted her on St. Barts. In self-defense, she averted her gaze and hugged his blazer tighter while she dug her free hand into the pocket of her slacks. Clearing her throat, she started for the stairs. "I'll get you that towel," she murmured, running ahead.

Oliver indulged her, though his hand had begun to dry on its own. She was nervous. Hell, so was he. God bless the sump pump for giving him entrée into the house; he hadn't been in the mood for picking locks tonight. It was dark and rainy and he'd had a long and trying day, not the least of which related to his anticipation of this visit. He'd planned it this way . . . almost. He'd guessed that she'd be better left alone for a while to quiet down, to put things into perspective. The kitten, the violets . . . they were simply reminders that he'd been thinking of her. Now came the test.

"Here you go," Leslie said as she handed him the towel. Then, not knowing what else to do, she stood back against the kitchen counter and waited for him to speak.

Unsure as to how he'd be received, Oliver was in no rush. He wiped his hands, rolled down his shirt sleeves, picked up his blazer from the chair over which Leslie had laid it and put it on.

Leslie's pulse raced as, arms hugging her waist, she followed each step of the dressing process. Damn, but he was handsome. Had he been this good-looking on St. Barts? His hair seemed darker; but of course it was wet. And the silver streaks seemed to have acquired several companions at his sideburns; or was that simply the reflection of her kitchen light? He looked leaner, which puzzled her, since she'd have thought that clothes would have made him look heavier. Perhaps it was the flattering fit of his gray slacks, the length of his legs, the thinning effect of the navy blazer he was slipping on. Beautiful material. Well tailored. But then, with his broad shoulders and tapering physique he was the perfect mannequin.

"There," he said with a final tug to his shirt cuffs. "Thank you."

"Thank *you*. I might have had a flooded basement had it not been for you."

"You'd have called a plumber," he said dismissingly. "It was a simple enough problem to solve."

"Well," she sighed, rubbing her hands together, "thanks anyway." She looked up at him, then away, intimidated by the intensity of his gaze. She didn't know what to say. She didn't know what she wanted to say. Oh, yes, she was glad to see him again. Even now, mired in confusion, she felt more alive than she had in five weeks. Why was he here? What did he want? At one time she might have believed that he wanted to be with her. Now she was wary.

"How've you been, Leslie?"

"Okay." She looked up shyly. "Thanks for the kitten. It's adorable. And the flowers." Her gaze wandered to the table where now only the empty vase stood. "They were beautiful."

"So are you."

Frowning, she absently rubbed at a small chip on the edge of the Formica countertop. Seeing her discomfort, Oliver instantly changed tactics.

"Listen," he said, clearing his throat, "I thought maybe we could go out for a bite."

"It's pouring."

"I don't mind if you don't. It's been a long time since lunch. Didn't I pass a place about ten minutes back down the road?"

She nodded, biting her tongue. She could fix dinner here. But she wouldn't. Oliver Ames in her cozy kitchen would be far too much for one Leslie Parish to endure.

"How about it?"

She shrugged. "I don't know."

"Have you eaten already?"

"No."

"Then come on." He cocked his head toward the front of the house. "Keep me company. We'll just get something to eat...and then talk. I'll drop you back here afterward." When she hesitated still, he tipped his head and eyed her teasingly. "You're not frightened of me, are you?"

"Frightened of you? Are you kidding?" She was scared to death, though quick to point out to herself that technically she hadn't lied. She could play that game, too.

"Then why not dinner?"

Because being with you may be as painful as being without you. On the other hand.... She sighed her resignation. "Why not."

Within fifteen minutes they were seated across from each other at the steak-and-sandwich place Oliver had selected. Leslie remained quiet, letting Oliver take the lead. If he wanted to talk, let him do the talking for a change. She'd done her share on St. Barts.

As though understanding her silent request, he began to speak soon after their orders were taken. And if he'd been hesitant to discuss himself during their time on the island, he was no longer. Indeed he seemed to want her to know everything. In turn, Leslie couldn't help but respond to his openness.

"I always wanted to be a doctor," he began quietly, almost shyly. "From the time I was a kid. It wasn't until I was nearly done with medical school that I decided on psychiatry."

"Why?"

"Why did I wait that long?" He gave a self-conscious laugh. "Because I think I wanted to see myself in a more—" he frowned as he searched for the word "—flamboyant field. I'd had my heart set on surgery. I was going to be a surgical pioneer, improving on existing transplant processes, experimenting with others."

"What happened?"

"My surgical rotation was a disaster. Not only was I clumsy with a knife, but I also discovered that I wasn't terribly sorry about the fact. Scalpels are cold, impersonal, sterile tools. The major tool the psychiatrist uses is his own intellect—I kind of liked that. I felt there was that much more of a challenge in psychiatry. Perhaps not the glory of a transplant surgeon. But a good feeling right here." He tapped his chest in the region of his heart.

"Has the good feeling persisted?"

"For the most part. Sure, there are some patients who are either beyond my help or, for one reason or another, resistant to it, but I've seen progress."

"Diane seems better," she began on impulse, then caught herself. "I'm sorry. I know you can't talk about her."

"That's all right. It wouldn't be violating doctor-patient confidentiality for me to say that things are beginning to move. She's opening up." His brow furrowed. "She calls me often, which is normal for someone just making that transfer of trust. I don't want her growing too dependent, though. I'd been seeing her three times a week; I've just cut it back by a session."

"She sounds okay when I speak with her."

"She is. She really is. And she'll be fine."

Leslie nodded, thinking how ironic it was that Diane might trust Oliver so completely while she had to remain on her guard all the time. Maybe she was the one with the problem, she mused, then reminded herself that it was the truth. To sit with Oliver like this, loving him so very much yet trying to remain detached, was pure hell.

"You enjoy private practice, then?" she asked, needing to keep the conversation going as a detour from her thoughts.

The waitress brought a carafe of wine, from which Oliver proceeded to fill their glasses before answering. "I do. . . ."

His slight unsureness caught her ear. "You don't sound sure."

"I am," he said more firmly, but he continued to study the swirl of rosé in his glass. "I'm not sure I see myself doing it forever." When Leslie remained silent, he went on. "I'm on the Bellevue—N.Y.U. staff; I spend two mornings a week there seeing patients. In some ways I prefer that kind of practice."

Leslie was puzzled. In the social circles in which she'd grown up, private practice would certainly have been far more prestigious, not to mention lucrative. "Why?"

"The patients. The problems. They're more diverse, often more extreme. I'm needed—and appreciated—that much more. Those patients could never afford the hourly rates I usually charge." His was a straightforward statement, devoid of either pride or arrogance. Perversely itching to find the latter, Leslie prodded.

"If you don't find private practice as rewarding, why do you do it at all? Bellevue is a teaching hospital; surely they'd take you on full-time."

"They would."

"Then why not?"

His eyes held hers levelly. "The money. I want the money private practice can offer."

So he was like the rest, she decided, though she felt no elation at having discovered his fault. "That's noble," she murmured.

"Not noble. Just practical." His eyes pierced her shell of cynicism. His voice held conviction. "I want a wife... and a family. I want to be able to support them well, to have a nice home, to travel, to take them to fine restaurants and the theater, to buy them gifts. I've been saving money for the last ten years, investing it, reinvesting dividends. The way I figure it, another seven or eight years should do it. Then I will be able to accept a full-time position at a hospital, either Bellevue or another, without denying my family... or myself."

For a minute Leslie had nothing to say. He'd been blunt. And honest. She couldn't believe that he would have risked evoking what he knew to be her distaste for the calculated amassing of money had what he said not been the truth. To her amazement, she respected him.

"Tell me about your family, Oliver," she said with a new note of interest in her voice.

And he did. He told her of his parents and sister, of their modest roots and the relative comfort they'd finally achieved. Over thick steaks and hearty salads, he told her of his college years, inspiring laughter and sympathy in turn.

That weekend, over dinner at a more elegant restaurant in the city, he told her more about his work, outlining a day in his life, amusing her with the zaniest of his cases.

The following Tuesday, as they sat, heads together, in a dim theater waiting for the movie to begin, he told her about his experience as an expert witness in criminal cases and about the book he hoped to write.

The Saturday after that, strolling arm in arm with her through a sprawling suburban shopping mall, he told her about his few good friends, his addiction to tennis, his dream to one day charter a boat and cruise the Mediterranean.

And the next Monday he insisted on taking her to the reception her sister Brenda was throwing to commemorate the debut of the Parish Corporation's home-computer system. Leslie hadn't wanted to go. Receptions such as these, to which only the shiniest of brass and the biggest and most promising of clients were invited, bored her to tears. Between Brenda and Oliver, however, she hadn't stood a chance. As it happened, with Oliver by her side through the entire ordeal, it wasn't all that bad. Indeed, the only awkward moment came when, as a couple amid several hundred, they ran into Diane and Brad. Diane seemed stunned, then embarrassed, then plainly nervous in their presence; Oliver handled the encounter with grace and tact. As for Leslie, she pushed the confrontation from her mind the instant they left the hall.

All in all, she was so in love with Oliver that she was ready to burst. He'd been so open, so gentle, so very obviously honest that she simply couldn't doubt him any longer.

She was also extremely frustrated. Through the

warm, casual getting-to-know-Oliver days, he never once repeated his words of love. After each date he'd drop her back at her house with a tender smile, perhaps even an affectionate hug, an extension of the hand-holding and elbow-hooking they did all the time. But though he had to have known she'd be more than willing, he didn't kiss her. Though her body seemed to ache endlessly for him, he showed no inclination to make love. And his words, other than to say that he'd call, were noncommittal.

Oh, he did call. Every night he called just to talk, to hear how her day had been, to tell her about his own. There were times when he was tired, when she could hear the fatigue in his voice, when it was her pleasure to be able to hear out his tale of woe, to commiserate, to soothe.

But he didn't say he loved her. And, fearing the breach of that last bastion, she said nothing.

"Hi, sweetheart."

"Hi."

"Good day?"

"Mmm. Busy. Three kids got sick and had to be sent home. Two of them needed rides to relatives without cars, so guess who drove. I did interview that woman for next fall, though. She's lovely."

"Think she'll be good with the kids?"

"She seemed it. I let her cover for me while I played chauffeur, then when I got back I was able to watch her in action. She's very warm."

"What's her background?"

"She just got a degree in special ed."

"No work experience?"

"Yeah. Six children of her own. Hey, how're *you* doing?"

"Not bad."

"Come on. You can do better than that. I thought the head banger at the hospital quieted down?"

"He did. A new one's into tap dancing."

"Tap dancing? You've got to be kidding."

"I'm not. Listen, babe. About the weekend. Should we, uh, should we try for the Berkshires again?"

"Do you want to?"

"Yes! But only if you do."

"I do."

"Good. Six on Friday?"

"Make it six-fifteen—I'm superstitious."

"Six-fifteen. I'll see you then."

"Sure thing. Bye-bye."

THEY NEARLY MADE IT. It was five-thirty when he called. His voice was as tense as she'd ever heard it. She instantly knew that something was very wrong.

"What is it, Oliver?"

"I've got a problem here. I may be late."

"You're at the office?" She could always pick him up there.

"No."

"At the hospital?"

"No."

He'd been so forthright in the past weeks. His evasion only fueled her concern. "What's wrong?"

In other circumstances, Oliver would have simply named a later time when he'd pick her up. But he knew all too well that his tenuous relationship with Leslie was based largely on openness. "It's Diane, Les," he offered quietly. "She's acting up again."

"Oh, no! What's she doing?"

"It's all right, sweetheart. She's just being. . .difficult."

"You're there now?"

"Yes. Listen, this may take a while. Why don't I call you when I have some idea what's happening."

"Oliver—"

"Please, Les," he begged, "no more questions now. I've been looking forward to tonight since...since St. Barts. And if you think I'm pleased with Diane's sense of timing, you're crazy." She heard his desperation. "Let me call you?"

"Okay."

"And Leslie?"

"Mmm?"

"I love you."

"I love you, too."

There was a pause, then Oliver's broken, "I'll call."

With tears in her eyes, Leslie hung up the phone. He'd sounded awful. What could possibly have happened? *I love you*, he had said. And she'd answered him with total openness for the first time herself.

Likewise, for the first time, she felt no confusion at all. Suddenly everything Oliver had said and done made sense. She believed him. She trusted him. And she knew precisely what she wanted to do.

Within half an hour she arrived at Diane's. To her dismay, the driveway was packed. She recognized the Weitzes' cars, Tony's car, Oliver's car...was that Brenda's car? She bit her lip as she pulled in behind one she didn't recognize. What was going on?

A frazzled Brenda opened the door. "Leslie! What are you—"

"What are *you* doing here?"

"I'm...I'm trying to help out."

Leslie strode past her into the hall and dropped her coat on a chair. Keeping her voice low, she looked around. "Where are they? What's she done? Why wasn't I called?" At the sound of raised voices in the living room, she headed that way.

"Leslie, please—" Brenda tried to stop her but it was too late. No sooner had Leslie appeared on the threshold than every eye turned her way.

What she saw, perplexingly enough, was what looked to be a very orderly family gathering. There was sign of neither destruction nor tears, though the level of tension in the room was up near the danger mark. Diane, wearing a look of placid arrogance, sat regally in a high-backed chair, while her husband stood behind her, a hand on either sculpted post, an indignant expression on his face. One end of the sofa was occupied by a man Leslie had never seen before. To her eye, his hair was too perfect, his three-piece suit too flashy, his entire bearing too glossy; she disliked him instantly. Tony stood by the fireplace in a state of obvious agitation. And Oliver stood by the window observing the group from a more detached position. His composure was, for show, well intact. Only Leslie recognized the grim set of his lips, the shadow of worry on his brow, the stiffness of his casual stance.

It was to Oliver that she spoke, her voice a whisper. "What's going on here?"

"You shouldn't have come—" he began somberly, only to be interrupted by an irate Diane.

"And why not? The rest of the family knows. And *she* should know. More than anyone, perhaps. After all, she's the one who's been mooning over you. I think she's got a right to the—"

"Diane!" Tony broke in. "That's enough!"

Diane fumed, her eyes blazing. "She'll know when it hits the papers anyway. She's your sister. Don't you want to make it easier for her?"

"Make what easier?" Leslie asked, her stomach tied up in knots. "What are you talking about?" Her wide-eyed gaze swung back to Oliver for a minute. His lips were tight.

Brad's were not. "It seems that your boyfriend has made good use of his high-priced time to seduce my wife."

Leslie stared, aghast. *"What?"* She was aware of Brenda coming up from behind to give her support, but shrugged off the hand at her shoulder.

It was Tony who took over, speaking more quietly. "Diane is threatening a malpractice suit against Oliver. She claims that he forced sexual relations on her for the sake of therapy."

"That's the stupidest thing I've ever heard," Leslie stated with amazing calm. "Oliver wouldn't do a thing like that."

"And I'd lie?" Diane cried, rejoining the fray. "See. He's got you as brainwashed as he had me. Only I'm not so crazy about him that I can't think straight."

Leslie swallowed hard and tucked her fists in her pockets. "That's a whole other issue. What does Oliver say to all this?"

Oliver's voice came deep and firm. "He denies it."

"Well, he can deny it in court," Brad countered, then cast a nod toward the slick man on the sofa. "We've retained Henry to represent us."

Leslie shook her head in disbelief. "You're serious! I'm amazed. You should know better, Brad. My God, it's not as though Diane's been the most stable—"

"Leslie!" Oliver cut in sharply, then lowered his voice. "Please."

The eyes that held hers said far more. *She's sick. Go easy on her. Besides, she hasn't got a case. Trust me. I love you.*

With the ghost of a nod, she walked to a free chair and sat down. She'd be quiet, but she'd be damned if she'd leave.

"Okay," Tony said with a tired sigh. "Where were we?"

Brad spoke up, looking down at his wife with a warmth that made Leslie nauseated. "Diane was just going through things chronologically. You were saying, sweetheart—"

"But what's the point of all this?" Brenda burst out, her gaze sliding from Brad to Diane and back. "I don't understand what you want. You're going to sue for damages? Neither of you needs the money."

Brad's jaw was set at a stubborn angle. "It's the principle of the thing. He's hurt our marriage and seriously threatened Diane's peace of mind."

"Now wait a minute," Oliver came forward. "Your marriage was on the rocks before I ever came on the scene. And as for Diane's peace of mind, it was nonexistent even then. Why do you think she spent an entire day cutting your bedroom to shreds?"

"That's beside the point," Brad went on in the way of the injured innocent. "What I'm concerned about is what happened *after* she started seeing you."

"But a judge and jury will take in the entire picture," Oliver pointed out calmly. "They'll ask about your marriage. They'll hear testimony about Diane's emotional state. Are you sure you want to put your wife through that?"

"For the satisfaction of seeing you lose your license to practice? Yes."

"That won't happen, Brad. Your allegations are absurd. You haven't a shred of evidence—"

"Other than my wife's testimony. Henry tells me that judges today lean heavily in favor of a woman who's been raped."

"She wasn't raped," Oliver scoffed impatiently. "Scandal is all you'll be able to create. Headlines. Innuendo. But no case."

Diane spoke softly. "Headlines and innuendo will be enough." She turned her smile on Leslie and crinkled up her nose. "Won't want to be seen with a guy who's got an atrocious reputation and no job, will you?"

"You're crazy," Leslie murmured.

"Di," Brenda said, "don't you think you're carrying this a little too far? I mean, headlines and innuendo could be harmful to the corporation, too."

"Not if I'm the injured party."

"But you're not," Tony injected, growing as impatient as Oliver, "and Brenda's right. This is foolish—"

"It is not!" Diane screamed. "You weren't the one who was—who was violated!"

Tony's tone mellowed to one of sweet sarcasm. "And you were truly violated?"

"Yes!" She tipped up her chin. "He took advantage of me! Maybe he takes advantage of every pretty girl who comes along. I don't know. That's something for the authorities to investigate." She arched a brow. "All I know is what he did to me."

"What did he do to you?" Brenda asked bluntly. "Tell us, Di. Tell us everything."

"He seduced me in the name of psychiatric treatment."

"Sounds like you got that from last month's *Post*."

"He did. He seduced me."

"Seduced—what does that mean?"

"Brenda . . . !" Diane protested in a whine.

"Seduced. Explain."

For the first time, Diane seemed to waver. "He . . . he . . . made love to me."

"Where?" Brenda shot back.

"Now just a minute," Henry the lawyer spoke up, Leslie thought his voice was as phony as the rest of him. "I don't believe my client has to answer your questions."

Brenda came forward, her hands on her hips. "Your client happens to be my sister. And the man she's accusing is a man who means one hell of a lot to my other sister. I'll ask whatever questions I want." She turned back to Diane. "Well? Where did you two make love?"

Diane shifted in her seat, keeping her gaze far from Oliver. "He made love to me, and it was in his office."

"On the desk?" Brenda came back as sweetly and sarcastically as Tony had moments before.

Diane scowled. "No." Her voice wavered. "There's a sofa there."

"Do you lie on the sofa during your sessions?"

"No. I . . . I sit in a chair."

"So how did he get you to the sofa?"

Diane grew petulant, reminding Leslie of a child who'd been caught in a lie and was trying to lie her way out of it. "He told me I'd feel better if I were to lie down."

"So you did."

"He was the doctor. Yes."

"And he just told you to take off your clothes?"

"Wait a minute—" Brad cut in, only to have Tony cut him off in turn.

"Let her answer. This is getting interesting."

"It's getting personal," Brad argued.

Tony's nostrils flared. "Isn't the whole thing personal?" Sucking in a loud breath, he turned to Brenda. "Go on."

Without pause, she resumed her relentless prodding. "What did he do . . . after you stretched out on the couch?"

Diane looked at the carpet. "He . . . he told me . . . ." She waved a hand and winced. "You know."

"I don't. Tell me."

"He said . . . ." She scowled in frustration. "You can imagine what he said, Brenda! What does any man say when he sets out to seduce a woman?"

Brenda pursed her lips. "I've only known two men in my life, and neither of them has tried to seduce me on a psychiatrist's couch. So my imagination's no good, Di. Tell me what he said."

Diane seemed to hesitate. She frowned, then gripped the arm of the chair. "He said sweet things."

"Like what?"

If Brenda's patience was wearing thin, Diane's was exhausted. With a sudden fury, she glared at her sister. "He told me it would be good for me, that it was a vital part of my treatment! He told me that he wanted me anyway, and that he'd make it good!" Her anger took on a touch of sadness. "He said that Brad must have been crazy to pass me by and spend time with women who couldn't possibly hold a candle to me."

Tears in her eyes, she bolted up. She was oblivious to the contorted expression on her husband's face. "He told me that I was still young and beautiful. That he loved me," she blurted defiantly. "And I loved him. He was kind and considerate and caring." Standing rigidly, she sent Leslie a gloating stare. "He's a good lover, Leslie. Very skilled and gentle. Not selfish like Brad," she spat.

Then, as the others watched in varying stages of anger, dismay and pity, she sank into her chair and let her head loll back. Astonishingly, her voice gentled along with her expression. She seemed to enter a dream-like state. "His skin was smooth here, rough there. And he was lean and hard. He wanted me. He did. And I wanted him." She closed her eyes and breathed deeply. "I think I'll always remember that smell. . . ."

Leslie sat forward. "What smell?" she whispered, entranced by her sister's performance.

Diane opened her eyes and sent Leslie a patronizing smile. "His cologne. Homme Premier." She shook her head. "He's so handsome. It's not every girl who's lucky enough to have a model as a therapist."

"He doesn't wear cologne," Leslie stated quietly.

"Excuse me?" Henry asked, twisting to study her.

She looked him in the eye and spoke slowly, with confidence. "I said that he doesn't wear cologne. I know. I spent a week with him at the villa on St. Barts." Rising smoothly, she walked to where Oliver stood and slipped her arm around his waist. Together they faced the gathering. "I know him far better than Diane ever will. Oliver doesn't wear Homme Premier...or any other cologne, for that matter. He never has. And if I have any say in the matter—" she looked adoringly up at him "—he never will." A slow smile found its way to her lips as a foil for the tears in her eyes. "He smells far too good on his own." Then, at the urging of his arms, she turned fully into his embrace. "I love you," she mouthed.

The moisture that gathered at the corner of his eye only enchanted his silent echo of the words. Then he smiled, and Leslie knew that everything would be fine.

10

FASCINATED, LESLIE STOOD staring at Oliver's sleeping form. He was magnificent. Dark wavy hair, mussed by loving, fell across his brow. His jaw bore the faintest shadow of a beard. His nose was straight, his lips firm. Lying amid a sensual array of sheets that barely covered one leg, and that part she now knew so well, he was the epitome of health, good looks and raw masculinity.

Again and again her gaze returned to the taunting strip of flesh at his hip. It would always excite her, even now that her fingers had repeatedly conquered its velvet smoothness. With a sultry half smile, she let her eye creep back up, over the broad and sinewed expanse of his lightly haired chest, to his face.

"Where've you been?" he murmured sleepily, holding out an arm in invitation for her to join him.

Flipping off the bathroom light, she was across the room and in his arms, stretched out against him, in seconds. "I was just looking at you," she said softly, "remembering the very first time I saw you."

"On St. Barts?"

"In *Man's Mode*. You were so beautiful. Tony must have thought I was crazy. I kept staring at that ad, at the expression on your face." She nestled her chin atop the soft hair on his chest. "You wore such a look of vulnerability; you seemed lonely and in love. I wanted to reach out to you then!"

"Took you long enough," he chided, giving her a squeeze.

Her voice was mellow. She kissed his warm skin, then laid her ear against it. "I know."

"What was it, Les? What finally brought you back to me?"

Surrounded by the night sounds of the Berkshires, she pondered his question. It had been long after dark when they'd arrived, so she'd been unable to see the beauty of the hills. But the sounds—the rustle of wind through the forest, the murmur of nocturnal life along its mossy floor, the occasional hoot of an owl—gave her a sense of well-being.

"I think I never really left you," she confessed, experimenting with the fit of her hand to his ribs. "I was so in love with you on St. Barts. I'd never known anything like that before!"

"You should have told me."

"Did you tell me?"

"No. But that was because I knew I'd been deceiving you, and I felt like a louse. The last thing I wanted was to tell you I loved you, then, when you learned the truth about what I did, have you throw the words back in my face. With regard to those three little words, I needed you to believe me."

"I believed you. Oh, I tried not to. But I believed you."

"You said you didn't."

"I lied. I was angry and hurt. I felt so . . . naive. I'd had a complex all along about having to compete with the glossy women I'd assumed you were used to. Then when I found out that you were a psychiatrist . . . ."

"Do you mind?"

"Mind what?"

"That I'm a psychiatrist."

"Of course not. What's to mind?"

In the darkness she could just make out the gleam in his eye. "Psychiatrists are loonies, didn't you know? They're as crazy as their patients. They're—" he curled his mouth around and drawled the word "—strange."

"Not this one."

"You're sure?"

"I'm sure. You must be nearly as rational as my sister Brenda." When he eyed her as though she were the strange one, she explained. "Your plan. It was brilliant. Those weeks you left me alone were awful. I missed you so terribly and kept trying to convince myself that I was better without such a lying devil, but it didn't work. When you sent that little kitten, I was overjoyed." Her voice dropped. "I love the kitten, Oliver."

"I'm glad," he whispered against her brow. His fingers idly traced the line of her spine. Her skin was warm and smooth; he'd never get his fill of touching her. "I had it all worked out. I figured I'd give you time to cool off and even miss me, then I'd let you get to know the real me. Then I'd bring you up here and start the seduction all over again." He paused. "But it was going to be slow and considerate, not fast and furious. I think I miscalculated somewhere along the way."

"There'll be other times for slow and considerate. Tonight I needed fast and furious. How did you know?"

"I couldn't control myself! I mean, it's tough for a man to be so turned on by a woman and not be able to go through with it."

"But you never even kissed me!" she protested, eyeing him in surprise. "You never gave the slightest indication that you wanted anything more than a squeeze or a hug."

"That was all part of the plan," he scoffed. "Let me tell you, you were gonna get it one way or the other over the weekend. Maybe it was good that Diane pulled her little act. She certainly brought things to a head."

His words gave them both food for thought. Leslie rubbed her cheek against his chest. He pulled her more tightly against him. Their voices were soft and intimate.

"Oliver, will she be all right?"

"I think so. I gave Tony a name of a colleague of mine who's very good. He'll be better able to treat Diane than I ever could."

"Why did she do that?"

"Ironically, it was probably her seeing us together at Brenda's reception that did it. It's not an uncommon phenomenon for a woman patient of a male doctor—in any kind of therapy—to think she's in love with him. She sees him as the source of her health, her confidence, her general well-being. I'd already begun to feel that Diane was growing too dependent on me; I told you that."

"I remember."

"I had just cut her sessions back from three a week to two. That may have bothered her. Brad was obviously still bothering her. He's a bastard." The aside was muttered under his breath. "A good deal of the time she feels she is unwanted and unloved. When she saw us together and, from what Brenda says, looking very much in love, she was jealous. Furiously jealous. Jealous of you. Furious at me. And Brad—well, with her cock-and-bull story she thought she'd be giving him the message that someone did want her, even if he did not."

"I feel so badly for her."

He drew soothing circles on her back. "So do I. She's very unhappy. I told Tony that I thought she and Brad should separate. Even her original outburst didn't faze Brad; Diane says that he's still seeing some little sweetie, and I think I believe her."

"Poor Diane. And we've got so much."

He hugged her, his arms trembling. "We do."

They lay together in silence for several minutes, each simply enjoying the presence of the other.

"Oliver?"

"Mmm?"

"How did you get to Diane's tonight? I mean, I'm surprised that she'd have wanted to give you a chance to defend yourself."

"She didn't. But she needed some sense of power, so she called Tony to tell him what she'd planned. He called me, then Brenda. He knew their lawyer was going to be there and hoped to nip the whole scheme in the bud."

"Why wasn't I called?" Leslie asked in a small voice.

Oliver planted a gentle kiss on her nose. "We didn't want you to be hurt. Diane's claim was pretty ugly."

"But it was false!"

"I knew that, but the words would have been hurtful enough. Besides, if we were successful, you'd never have been any the wiser to her threat." He paused then, hesitant. "Leslie?"

"Mmm?"

"Did you ever believe her?"

She brought her head up in surprise. "Believe Diane? Of course not. Were you worried?"

"That you'd believe her, a little. After what I'd done to you on St. Barts, I wasn't sure how far your trust would go."

"Were you worried that she would bring the case to trial?"

"I wouldn't be honest if I didn't say yes. She was right in a way. Headlines and innuendo could have easily damaged my career. Not destroyed it, but damaged it badly. Even if a person is found not guilty by a jury, the stigma of having been accused in the first place remains. It's a sad fact, one that our system of justice can do little to change." He grew quiet, pensive, his breathing even, close to her ear. Hooking his foot around her shin, he drew her leg between his and pressed her hips more snugly to him. Then he held her still, appreciating the beauty of the moment. "Thank you, Leslie," he said at last, his voice intensely gentle.

"For what?"

"For trusting me."

She laughed shyly. "It's nothing. You're an easy one to trust," she pinched his ribs, "even when you are lying through your teeth."

"I don't lie!" he stated with such vehemence that she realized he would always be sensitive about what had happened on St. Barts. She couldn't deny her delight; somehow she had managed to find the most straightforward man in the world.

"I know," she apologized gently. "I was only teasing." Then she grew more thoughtful herself. "A little while ago you asked what had brought me back to you. It was several things, I think. Time, for one. I was able to sort things out, to put things into perspective. I realized that what you'd said made sense. And I missed you so much I was very willing to give you any benefit of the doubt.

"When we started to see each other and I got to know you, I saw that what you'd said was right. Model or psychiatrist, you were the same man underneath. You were so open then, making up for all you hadn't said on the island. And right about that time I was beginning to feel like a hypocrite."

"You? A hypocrite?"

"Mmm." She breathed in his natural scent and was buoyed up by it. "For all my talk, I really wasn't any more honest with you—or myself—than I'd accused you of being. I did love you. I loved you back on St. Barts. When we made love, well, I played games with myself. I told myself that the only thing that mattered was the moment, that I didn't care about the past or the

future. But I did. I should have been more open about
my feelings then. I should have let you speak when I
knew you wanted to." She raised soulful eyes to his. "It
was my fault that you didn't tell me about yourself. But
I was afraid—afraid of what you might say, afraid that
it might burst the bubble of illusion we'd created. It was
such a lovely bubble. I didn't want anything to happen." She looked down. "So you see, I was pretty bad
myself. I created an illusion and clung to it as it suited
me. But I was fooling myself to think that I could return
to New York and forget you. I realized that during the
cab ride home from the airport."

Oliver skimmed her cheek with the side of his thumb
and brought her chin up. "I love you, lady. Do you
know that?"

Seeing it written on every plane of his face, she smiled
and nodded. "You know," she whispered through a veil
of happy tears, "I feel sorry for all your female patients.
If you'd been my therapist, I'd have certainly fallen in
love with you."

"If you'd been my patient," he growled, rolling slowly
over to pin her to the bed, "I'd sure as hell have been
guilty of some mighty unethical thoughts."

"Only thoughts? No acts?"

"Nope."

"I'm not pretty enough? Or rich enough? Or thin
enough? Why not?"

"If you want to know the truth, that sofa happens to
be the most uncomfortable thing I've ever been on!"

"Oh? So you have . . . tried it out?"

He nipped her shoulder in punishment. "I've sat on it.
I've fallen asleep on it once or twice."

"Have you ever *made love* on it?"

"No. Maybe we'll try it sometime."

"Aw, I don't know, Oliver. That might feel . . . unethical."

"But you're not my patient."

"I know, but . . . ."

"Tell me you're tired of me already."

"Are you kidding? It's just . . . well . . . even though Diane won't be suing you, I think I'll always remember her threat. I'd feel guilty making love in your office. Your patients have problems so much more serious than ours. . . ."

Adoring her sensitivity, Oliver felt choked up. When he could finally speak, his voice was a husky murmur. "You're amazing, you know that?" Before she could answer, he sealed her lips with his own in a kiss so gentle and loving that she could have wept for all she did have. "It doesn't bother you then," he mused against her mouth, "that I'm a psychiatrist?" He was thinking of her mother and what Tony had told him.

She sent her tongue in search of the corner of his lip, then smiled. "I'm proud of you."

"You will have to meet my parents," he quipped, recalling an earlier discussion about pride.

She remembered too and blushed. "I did wonder for a while there what kind of parents would be proud to have a gigolo for a son. Now that I know better, I'd love to meet them."

"And you'll marry me?"

"I'd love that, too."

He sucked in his breath, then let it out slowly as he raked the length of slender flesh beneath him. "You are beautiful. Not too thin. Not too rich. Just right. When we get back to the city I'm going to buy you a silky white negligee. I'd love to be able to take it off. . . ."

"Oliver!" she exclaimed, delighted by the very definite effect the simple thought of it had on him. "You must have this thing for nudity. What would Freud say about that?"

He moved more fully on top of her. "I don't give a damn. Freud was nothing but a constipated old—"

"Shhhhh. . . ." She put a finger to his lips, then let it wander to his hairline, into the thick waves, around his ear to trace that silver arc. "I like nudity, too. Knowing that you were naked beneath that sheet in your ad nearly drove me crazy. Oliver?"

He managed a muffled, "Uh huh?"

"Will you stop. . .doing that for a minute so. . .I can speak?"

"Doing what?"

"Moving like that." He'd begun to shift against her on the pretense of kissing her eyes, then withdrawing, kissing her nose, then withdrawing, kissing one earlobe, then the other. In essence his entire body was rubbing her in all the right places, and she'd begun to sizzle.

He stopped instantly, propping himself above her. "There. Better?"

Was frustration better? "Not really. . .except for speaking."

"So. . .what were you going to say?"

"I wanted to, uh, to ask you a favor."

"Shoot."

She raised her hands to his shoulders and followed their progress as they slowly descended over his chest. When her palms felt the unmistakable tautness of his nipples, she stopped. "It's about your modeling. When we're married. . . ."

"What is it, sweetheart?"

She shot him a glance, then retreated. "I know it's silly of me to even think of this—"

"Out with it, woman, so we can get on with it!"

"I don't want you posing nude! I don't think I can stand it! I don't want other women seeing your body! I want you all to myself!" Running out of breath, she lowered her voice. "I told you it was silly."

"It's not one bit silly, Leslie," Oliver returned gently.

"It's sweet and loving and possessive, and it pleases me tremendously."

"Really?" she asked timidly.

"Really."

"Because I love your body." She slid her hands from his chest and ran them down his sides to his thighs. "I do love your body." Lifting her head, she pressed her lips to the turgid spot that her palm had just deserted.

"It's yours!"

"Just like that?"

"Just like that. There's just one little catch."

"Uh oh. Here it comes." She shut her eyes tightly. "Okay. Tell me."

"I want *your* body. That's a fair exchange, isn't it?"

"I suppose."

"What do you mean, 'you suppose'? You're supposed to be ecstatic."

"But . . . what about my mind? Don't you want that, too?"

"Your mind? Oh. That. Uh, well, let's see. We could always put it in a little box on the nightstand—hey, that tickles!"

"The ad was right, you know. You *are* a rogue."

"Any objections?"

She smiled and spoke with confidence, serenity and love. "None at all, Oliver. None at all."

THE AUTHOR

Barbara Delinsky, a self-confessed idealist, believes that everyone's life is enriched by love. She has a lot of scope for love in her own life, with a husband and three growing sons. Her boys are in school, so she has time to write every day.

As well as writing, Barbara swims a mile every day, at the local Y. She and her husband love to travel, and the Caribbean is one of their favorite destinations. She decided one of the Caribbean islands would make a perfect setting for this book.

COMING NEXT MONTH FROM

Harlequin Temptation ™

BY MUTUAL CONSENT #5
Marion Smith Collins

When Toni Grey met fellow attorney Nick Trabert, she was smitten. Nick stirred her senses as no man ever had, but he was engaged to the one woman Toni would never dream of hurting....

THE FOREVER KIND #6
Alexandra Sellers

While on a solo "getaway" trip in the Canadian bush, actress Cady Hunter encountered devastating Luke Southam. They agreed to share a campsite that first night...a night that led to sharing far more.

CAST A GOLDEN SHADOW #7
Jackie Weger

Calico Jones trusted no man...until she rescued Irish McCaulley from a raging river. His tantalizing lovemaking brought her to the brink of ecstasy, but he soon wreaked havoc with her heart.

FOR NOW, FOR ALWAYS #8
Lynn Turner

Overwhelming passion had united the Hartmanns in marriage, but jealousy and misunderstanding had torn them apart. Eight years later, a penitent Neil returned to reclaim his wife. Proud Lacey said no, but her treacherously aroused body said otherwise....

FOUR TEMPTING
NEW TITLES EVERY MONTH